fighting
gravity

fighting gravity

Peggy Rambach

STEERFORTH PRESS
SOUTH ROYALTON, VERMONT

For information about permission to reproduce
selections from this book, write to
Steerforth Press, L.C.
P.O. Box 70, South Royalton, Vermont 05068

LIBRARY OF CONGRESS CATALOGING-IN-PUBLICATION DATA

Rambach, Peggy.
　　Fighting gravity : a novel / Peggy Rambach.— 1st ed.
　　　　p.　cm.
　　ISBN 1-58642-023-2 (alk. paper)
　　1. Interfaith marriage—Fiction. 2. Conflict of generations—Fiction.
　　3. Traffic accident victims—Fiction. 4. Married people—Fiction.
　　5. Jewish women—Fiction. 6. New England—Fiction.
　　7. Novelists—Fiction. 8. Catholics—Fiction.
　　9. Alabama—Fiction. I. Title.
　　PS3568.A4395 F54 2001
　　813'.54--dc21
　　　　　　　　　　　　　　　　　　　　　　　00-012034

5050110024211 0

FIRST EDITION

For my mother,
Patricia J. Scharlin

and my father,
Harvey W. Rambach

acknowledgments

I'd like to extend my gratitude to the Massachusetts Cultural Council and the St. Botolph Club Foundation, whose grants in literature helped support the writing of this book. I am fortunate to have found all those at Steerforth Press and my editor Robin Dutcher's valued enthusiasm and advice. I am also deeply grateful to my agent, Loretta Fidel, who waited and waited and waited, and whose cry of Onward! always sustained me. And I want to thank all those who patiently, generously, and without fail helped scare away the doubts and demons, particularly Joan McIver, Ellie Dexter, Laura Pappano, Corbin Sexton, Jane Brox, Dorit Lammers, Janet Howell, Alexandra Marshall, Jeffrey Kelly, Françoise Rambach, J. Gary Taylor, the late Luke Taylor, and Denny Blodget, who has believed in me since I was a high school girl. And of course, I could not have done without my sweetest and most constant companions, Cadence and Madeleine, and "da Woo."

part one

one

She wondered if anyone recognized them. The ushers, the ticket sellers. No one seemed to. Not the one who looked familiar, who stood beside the ticket counter to rip tickets for every theater behind him because it was a slow weekday night. He was a young Hispanic man, with a flat-topped haircut, shaved close on the sides, a mustache she could see through. He was big shouldered, and he didn't fit too well into the light-blue polyester jacket he had to wear. He glanced down at her husband, then straight at her, putting the two together. She wondered if he'd been the one who'd once smiled at them and asked like a tavern keeper, what'll it be tonight, when some years back her husband had decreed every Monday movie night.

"Don't underestimate the importance of ritual," he'd told her, one of the many things he made her think about that she'd never thought about before. Ritual. But it was also his desire to never let a good thing go unrepeated. A good day fishing on a charter boat, and every summer ever after they had to do it again, a good party, and only a month or two later they gave another one. And after a good movie in an empty theater on a Monday night, he'd insisted they return every Monday night after. And she indulged him, amused, sometimes teasing, for he was like a child who pleads, *Again, Again,* certain he could recapture the very same pleasure felt from a moment already past.

Still, they had to have been considered regulars, going at least once a week over years, Monday or not. Even after their first daughter was born. And it had been one of the last things they'd done. Gone to see some silly romantic comedy. A forgettable movie for a night she would so often recall.

The girl at the concession stand gave them no sign either; maybe she was new, maybe not. She tried to remember her, black hair dyed that odd pinky-red that she supposed had said "copper" or "auburn" on the bottle. Like the other people around them, the girl only looked at him as they approached, but she knew it was not from recognition of the couple they'd been before.

Always unusual. She'd worn her thick blond hair waist length, parted just off center, same as when she was a seventies teenager who had worn platform shoes as well, bell-bottoms and a peasant blouse. He did not want her to ever cut it, so she never had. And he always wore some hat, a beret in winter and fall, or a wide-brimmed fawn-colored cowboy hat, or in summer, a straw fedora, and he wore, too, a full beard, thick and well-trimmed and permanent. He'd grown it when, just before Vietnam, he'd resigned from the Marine Corps and had never shaved it. And since she'd first known him, it had changed color from shades of red and brown to white, the white creeping down from his sideburns in increments, over years, like the slow maturation of fledgling feathers. He was twenty-two years older than she.

This had always drawn looks and people's wrong assumptions, which for a time she'd corrected with the kind of glee that comes from having played a successful practical joke. But then it had grown tiresome, maybe after their first daughter was born; and then, finally, she couldn't blame people for their error. The assumption was logical. They were less unusual, more freakish, even to her, after a time. And when the very first doctor made the predictable daughter mistake that very first night and said more defensively than apologetically, "You're very young," she simply replied, "I know."

"Small, plain popcorn, large Coke, Nestlé's Crunch," she said.

Still, no sign of recognition, but then it had always been he who gave this order, while she, uninterested in concession food, found them seats. But he was too low. Child's height, he looked now straight at the rows of candy bars of such unwieldy sizes that they looked magnified. He could not be anything else but slightly behind her, and she could tell he hurried to unhook from the chair handles the cheap green, canvas backpack she'd bought long ago at some army-navy store for an outing she couldn't remember, and had never imagined would be this one.

He dug into it for his wallet, to have the cash ready this time, because she'd paid for the tickets. She'd named the movie because even though she'd been standing behind him, the ticket seller had looked to her, and she'd been taken off guard, not quick enough, here, in a public setting, to indicate by not answering, or by rude instruction, that he, too, was capable of saying what movie they wished to see, and buying with his own money, the tickets, informing the ticket seller and everyone in line behind them, that her husband's seated position did not mean his brain was impaired.

But they both were not used to how long things took now, and so she'd paid, something she'd done before, yet now the act took on a significance she did not intend it to have, implied that she, like the ticket seller, judged him incapable of the task. And she'd imagined everyone watching, the ticket seller, the couple behind them, and her, watching him twist, unhook, unbuckle, open, take out, everyone watching, everyone waiting for him to complete something that had once taken seconds.

Now she was ordering, because she thought he'd feel foolish shouting up the steep slope of glass. Quickly she had to decide what was worse, and his lack of protest felt to her like acquiescence. Still, she was terribly relieved to take from his hand the ten dollar bill.

She gave him the change, which he threw loose into his backpack, both realizing then they'd not yet devised a new way for him to keep his coins. And she handed down to him the Coke, then the popcorn, and just placed the candy bar in his lap, feeling as she did so, that she felt like she was doing something else, and then she smiled, nearly laughed when she realized: loading a grocery cart.

She wanted to tell him because suddenly, amazingly, it could all become so comical, and she loved it when that happened. *We're so pathetic,* she'd screamed, both of them laughing until they gasped, had to wipe tears and blow their noses and then start laughing again, because eight-and-a-half-months pregnant, and he just home, she'd had to navigate a climb onto his raised, rented bed, and over his prone body, to lie beside him to watch a video. And just the thought of it, for days afterward, had made her smile.

But not tonight. He wore his new Marine fatigue cap, and the hair she could see at his temples looked sticky. His face was flushed, his baseball jacket snapped to the chin, the collar tight at his neck, pressing. All his clothes looked like that now that he'd gained enough weight back to fit into them again. But the fit was different, his shirts, jackets all looking now pushed up, or he squashed down into them. No longer was he just a man in children's clothing, the eccentric costumes she'd tease him about, his hats, cowboy snap-button shirts, and this jacket he loved so much, made of blue satin with the two big red socks stitched onto the left side, their texture that of the bumpy swatch on her older daughter's touch-and-feel book. Now it was children's clothing on a man's body confined. And there was nothing really funny in it, as though it had been forced on him for someone's sadistic pleasure, his face, his eyes, always, an unnerving contrast.

He looked past her, as if as long as he didn't look at her, he would not really be there. But his eyes were dark and they glittered, looking like they did when he was angry. She felt uncertain. She thought, not angry at her exactly. It was the look that followed the other one, the one he'd had when they'd gotten there, at the ticket counter, his eyes like those of a brown dog she'd seen long ago running between cars on a crowded ramp up to a city bridge. How he'd looked in the hospital when she'd decided he was able to see people and too many came at once, or at home when the same thing happened. There was no appeal in it, no fear, just a dreamy confusion, like he'd been deprived of oxygen. She knew her reassurance would be harmful, the way it is to wake a sleep-walker. He would be startled, he might scream or strike at her. In the hospital and at home she had gently shooed the people out, but she always kept her distance from him, waited for it to pass to this. This rage that she also knew not to approach, that he hoarded, would keep her from with raised lips and a snap, like it was some-thing he was feeding on.

A little afraid, she took up her position behind him, but knew it was not a solution either, for pushing him when he was like this became a taunt. And even if she'd chosen to walk beside him, as she had in the parking lot, even if she'd let him now control the chair's speed himself down the long, sloping theater aisle, she'd still be no better than the ticket seller, just like everyone else, no bet-ter than the general enemy whom he called "Bipeds."

"So what are you going to do with it?" he'd asked. "Pickle it?" Asking after the doctor explained how it would be done.

"Just like a chicken bone," the doctor had said, holding his hands up before his gold-rimmed glasses and twisting them in opposite directions. They had both groaned and laughed, the room full of celebration and relief because it had almost killed him.

She arrived one day during the third week to know immedi-ately something had changed from the day before. His face looked thinner, more exhausted, in a weirdly peaceful way, and bags of blood hung from the hook that had once held clear ones before his body had been able, finally, to provide for itself what they had. And all he needed was the shots, always the shots they both yearned for, watching the clock.

But never blood, and she heard that his had been all over the floor. She saw for herself one overlooked drip, dried like paint on the steel bed frame, left there like damning evidence. A young nurse on a routine four A.M. check had screamed and run to find another nurse who had turned out to be Gordon, their favorite, who left his smell of sweet aftershave and whatever he put in his pompadoured hair, behind him. And who would stop off in her husband's room on his break to peer down from the window to Emergency and announce who was dead or alive on their short trip from ambulance to entryway. They loved him, and his hands that could lift and turn and touch her husband's limbs in a way no one else could. It was he who'd clamped the artery before any doctor arrived.

"Just a floating bone chip," their doctor had said, so offhandedly that she was confused. Did he not want her to be alarmed? Or did he want to downplay it, so he could have a few more chances to save it, knowing they would, as they did, beg him to just take it off.

"I mean it looks like a fucking casserole," her husband had said to him.

Not a casserole, she thought. Just meat. Like a cow's, a pig's. Pale, red, and bloodless. Open from knee to ankle, gray bits of bone, flat and rough as shale, held fast in a crooked line, steel pins crisscrossed right through and attached to four horizontal bars. She said, "It's not often one can see the very bones of the man she loves," for she washed it everyday, the nurses being so busy, and she needing to do something for him, something besides sitting and knitting, and watching.

She could not touch him, or read to him, or even sing to him, as she had on the other floor, in the windowless room with no time, when his eyes were swollen to slits and his ability to speak taken away by the greater importance of his breath, given to him by the machine that reached his lungs through his mouth and throat, and so all he had were his hands and a red felt tip pen and a yellow pad, always remembering to write "please" after his requests. And sometimes *drowning,* it said. Drowning. So she sang to him, leaning close down to his ear. She had a good singing voice and now she used it like an additive to morphine and tranquilizers. Knowing it kept him calm, and her calm, through the

sudden bleating of machine alarms, his and all the still peoples'
around them that the nurses moved through like fish between
stones; slipping quickly, stopping, tapping, flicking switches, shaking tubes, touching metal, flesh, bringing, taking while she sang,
and looked at his chest. The mole just where his chest hair gave
over to smooth skin, his chest hair, thick and curly and swirled
white just at his solar plexus, reassured by this part of him that it
was still him.

But in this next room, she couldn't sing to him anymore. It was
not the room of survival as the first one was, but the one for heal-
ing, and the morphine barely touched what waited there for him.
The pain, which forbade her touch, too. A captor of them both,
his torturer, and her torture to watch. His task was only to be silent
and still, to make his concentration a kind of placation to save
himself. And so her songs, or her hands, broke this fragile defense.
And she could only sit, until she asked to do for him what the others had to do, hold the urinal, wash his hair, clean him and the
stainless steel pan — when finally his body got that part of it
working again — and clean the left leg, the one so hurt, it didn't
even hurt much. Not like the right one, strung up with ropes and
black cylindrical weights.

All of the pain in that leg collected in his perfectly unscathed
big toe, a phenomenon that could sometimes make them laugh,
his astonishment at the illogic of it, the blatant injustice of it. "My
fucking toe," he'd say. "My fucking toe," and asked for its removal
before he made his lower left leg the subject of this demand.

Because dying flesh doesn't hurt. And she knew the bath of peroxide the nurses had taught her to administer and the new gauze
she wrapped round the metal cage, the shiny wrenches in the tool-
boxes the orthopods carried, his repeated trips to surgery, were not
working. There was always more dead to take away. And she could
not believe there would be enough living left to ever stand on.

She said good-bye to his foot. Pretty and white, his feet were
small, and his toes crouched close in a perfect diminished line. And

she kissed his foot, feeling its waste, how wasteful it was that this part of him appearing as whole and healthy as it did when the leg above it was as well, had to go. "Poor little guy," she said to it. "Too bad you weren't the right." And they laughed. Still so relieved.

It meant he could go home soon, the right in a cast, looking finally like a normal broken leg, she'd said. And then a fake leg for the other. Kind of cool. Kind of cocky. Would look good with his leather jacket, baseball jacket, vests, hats, and cowboy boots. A sexy limp, she said. Canes the new accoutrement to collect along with his pipes.

Like it had been the hospital that kept him broken, and made the life they'd had before he went there something they could not retrieve. Until he came home. And then, like an explosion reversed, everything would fly back together again.

They stopped at a row three down from the center, just a little closer than most would prefer, their usual place, and when he leaned forward to put on his brakes, she heard the candy bar smack just beside the aisle carpet, onto the concrete floor. "Shit," he said. And she said, "I'll get it," realizing as she did, the words implied a choice. She walked around his chair, bumped her shin on the chair leg, always extended because his right leg could only bend sixty degrees. That's what the therapist measured with her compasslike gadget after each session she spent pushing firmly, steadily on his lower leg to bring it maybe up to eighty someday. But when she let go, the leg always sprang back with the resilience of a diving board.

She held his popcorn and Coke, while he put his candy bar in his coat pocket, and to her relief, unsnapped his coat and shucked it from his body the way he had when he'd driven. She handed him back the popcorn, the drink, and moved past him to sit in the aisle seat, the one he'd always chosen for himself. Now, in the aisle, he sat higher than she. The chair arm, attached to a flat, vertical square of metal, rose just next to her face. It was a reach, but she touched his hand, just as he raised it to perhaps scoop popcorn from the container he'd placed between his thighs, so the gesture seemed less one of affection, more like restraint. But she held on, and said, "Well, here we are." He didn't answer. "I'd say it's an accomplishment," she said. He squeezed her hand and let go. And though she couldn't see over his chair arm, she could tell he'd placed his hand on top of his popcorn container, and she remembered that that was what he did, never ate until the movie began, but put his hand on top, as though he were hiding the contents, or holding them in. And the gesture amused her and startled her a little. Its very familiarity making it odd. It might have been something she would have remembered about him back at the movies for the first time, had he died. And it felt a little like that to her now, as did many things, like something recalled, not real. And strange because it wasn't strange. As if nothing should have survived what they had, unaltered.

two

Gerard Babineau will be hit by a car on a clear summer night when he stops to help some people up there ahead. A woman, looks like, on the driver's side, a man just getting out on the passenger side of a car that's stuck full in the third lane. The taillight reflectors catch his beams. On the far right of the road two people have already stopped and are at the call box, conveniently right there. But the woman ahead of him is waving at him, definitely wants him to stop there for her and she looks a little hysterical, the way she's waving her arms. Then he sees she's got something on her face, a shadow, mud, pulling closer, blood. Blood of course, and he's a little shaken. He moves to the far left lane, downshifts, throws his cigarette out the open window, and turns off the country music station, which he realizes has been irritating him, too loud now that he's slowed. He passes the woman, and sees her face in his closed passenger door window as she bends to look in at him, pleading, still not convinced he will stop, though he's given every indication. He raises his hand, a quick salute of acknowledgment, reassurance, then flicks on the hazards, and bumps the left wheels up onto the curb of the grassy median.

They say they hit something. The woman does. The man keeps saying, *No hablo Inglese, no hablo Inglese*, as if this were the cause of their immediate difficulty. And Babineau, as he's called, a man called by his last name, his last name his first, wants to say, "It's all right, buddy, really," but the woman won't stop speaking, and her accent is strong, her syntax a little confused. He's got to concentrate to get the full picture. She keeps pointing under the car, and it becomes clear to him that they have hit something, that they have hit a motorcycle. That the motorcycle had not been moving, had not even been upright. It had been lying on its side, smack in the middle of the highway, like some piece of debris fallen from the bed of a truck.

They did not see the driver. Have not seen the driver. And he understands with a start, that that is why she is so worked up, pointing and pointing to a thick black puddle he sees spreading from under the car and right toward the tapered toes of his handmade cowboy boots.

He steps back. "Holy shit," he says and looks at the puddle, then up, and sees the man looking at him expectantly, apologetically, from across the roof of the car. Babineau would really like a cigarette and wishes he didn't always find himself in these predicaments; prying his wallet into the pink, foaming mouth of some guy having an epileptic fit on the main street of his town; standing between six punks to discourage them from beating each other up with baseball bats right outside his local bar. But once a Marine, always a Marine. He was not trained and had not trained others to stand gawking like your basic civilian.

But right now he is not feeling too eager to investigate the mess that might very likely be underneath the car. He thinks it would be better, anyway, now, to take the woman, who is bleeding and crying and shaking and who might be going into shock, to his car where he could sit her down, or lie her in the back, legs propped, and wrap her in his white jacket he has left folded in the front seat. He doesn't like the jacket, never did. Ties, jackets, ridiculous costumes. Make men look like penguins, he's always thought, and damn uncomfortable. This would be a good excuse to chuck the thing.

He hands the woman the bandana he keeps in his back pocket for a handkerchief. Thinks he should have thought to do that sooner, and then tells the man what he is going to do. The man's face turns both panicked and confused. Again, he says *No hablo Inglese, Signor.* He is a young man, and Babineau observes from the way the yellow shirt clings to his shoulders and biceps that he lifts weights, too. Babineau beckons to him, points to the woman, who he thinks maybe is not the guy's girlfriend, because of how the guy's just been standing there on the other side of the car, then points to where his own car is parked, and the young man smiles, nods, so relieved to comprehend, and walks down and behind and around the back of the car, and as he walks toward Babineau, Babineau sees behind him headlights, far away and approaching.

He thinks, good, and raises his arms and crosses and uncrosses them with wide, slow sweeps. He is glad. Marine or not, it would be a hell of a lot better to look under that car with someone else, someone who could speak English at least.

He keeps waving. The young man stops and turns to see. The woman is crying and holding the bandana to her face. And the car, all by itself on the nighttime highway is not slowing down. It is going as fast as any car would in the third lane of an empty highway at night were nothing there sitting big and stationary in front of it. So it looks to Babineau like no one is driving the car, like one of those crash tests, or like the driver must be suicidal, deliberately aiming to plow right into the back of this already banged-up, secondhand looking Pinto, and do more damage to the poor fucker who might be underneath. Babineau realizes then, that if this is going to be avoided, the driver had better swerve fast to the right. Or to the left.

"She swerved left," Trooper Jimmy Greer says to the wife later on that night. Really, early morning. He stands with her in front of the deserted reception desk in the lobby of a small, brand-new emergency medical facility, a place that more frequently handles men who've overexerted themselves behind lawn mowers or snowblowers, women having babies too fast, kids who've fallen out of trees, off bikes and swingsets. He'd known it was the guy's wife the moment she walked in, even though she looked young, very young, a lot younger than the guy, that was for sure. He was, of course, the only one injured who had a wife. But more than that, though, it was the jeans, the old sweatshirt, the kind of clothes someone would throw on if they'd been rousted out of bed by the kind of call she got. And it was her face. Scared, and excited, too. She didn't know what the hell was going on, only that it was not a good thing.

"Could have gone left. Could have gone right," he elaborates, and shakes his head and shrugs. Always there is that move, in any investigation. One small decision. A reflex. Like the way the eye shuts when something gets too close, too fast.

He has already told her about the rest. The people involved, the sequence of events. How they found her husband fully conscious, and talking. "Even joked with the EMT," he told her, "when he'd had to cut off his boot. Told him he better buy him another pair." She smiled and said, "Yes, he likes his boots."

He told her how they'd found the sister of the other man. He consulted his clipboard. An Anita Lorcas, sitting on the median. And with the exception of the cut on her head she sustained from the earlier collision, she was otherwise unharmed. "Ms. Lorcas said your husband threw her out of the way," he told her. "Not just a Good Samaritan, a hero, too." The wife, though, had just kept looking at him. "Really," he said. "Not a lot of people would do what your husband did." She nodded and smiled. Seemed she wanted him to just get on with the story, so he said they'd found the motorcyclist walking around dead drunk, in the lot of the industrial park right there off the highway. And that apparently he'd dumped the bike going about sixty miles per hour, "So inebriated," he said, "he just kind of bounced and rolled, got up, hardly a scratch, and left his bike. Left it there," he said. "Practically brand-new Kawasaki." He was still incredulous. Never heard of any owner of a bike treating it like garbage, drunk or not.

He told her that they found the woman who hit them, a Carol MacMillan, to be absolutely substance free. Just driving home from visiting a friend.

And that's when he got to the decision. The move. The turn of the steering wheel to the left instead of the right to avoid the Pinto, which had been just about gutted by the bike.

"And the other man? The woman's brother, you said? How is he?" she says, her voice calm, her eyes directly in his.

"Not so good," he says, and looks down, a little shake of the head, so she'll know and he won't have to say it flat out, like a violation of the poor son of a bitch's privacy.

She says, "Oh."

"The car." He looks back at her, and tells her it's at Garrity Wreckers in Wilmington. "I'm going to write the directions down for you."

"So it was wrecked?" she says, not sounding particularly dismayed, just needing to know things.

"No. No. The car," he says, "not a scratch," and shrugs again, smiles apologetically for the irony that she, no fool, catches.

"I guess maybe I should go in there to see him now," she glances to the room her husband is in, just off the lobby.

He sees she is being polite and says, "Of course," and apologizes for keeping her so long, lifts the pad he's going to write on from the counter of the reception desk, the kind that has the same cartoon at the top of every page, and tells her he'll give her the directions when she leaves. Then he watches her turn and walk toward the open doorway of the room and thinks how they don't often come alone like that. Always a mother, a friend with them. He looks at her hair, long and blond, heavy and a little tangled, and he thinks that, from behind, she could be about fifteen years old.

She sees what look like balloons. Not balloons. More like pool toys, floats, two inflated clear plastic cylinders that are where his legs should be. They protrude from the cluster of people who surround him. She has not expected to see anything like this, has never seen anything like it, and stops at the doorway. The room is small, and is crowded and busy and filled with a light as white and bright as a camera flash. She sees the white sheets on the stretcher mattress, clear glass bottles still swinging from where they've been hooked onto shiny steel stands, the white and bleach-green clothing, masks, and latex gloves of the people who surround him, one breaking away, then another, to write something down, to get something from a cabinet, and returning rapidly, as if they cannot safely remain separate for long.

Still, she stands in the doorway, not sure she should go in, afraid to be in the way, to disrupt, or interfere with the importance and urgency of what is happening in front of her. And though the trooper has told her this is where he is, she has not seen any part of him that is recognizable, so she cannot be certain.

"Mrs. Babineau?" A nurse says this to her, suddenly there, apart from the rest. And Ellie says, "Yes," although it is not her name. She does not, never has, considered his name to be another name for herself. It is only his, his French ancestors', the last name of his children and the last name of his first and second wives. Whenever she is called by it, she notices, but would not correct it now and only does so lately when someone is preparing to write it down.

"I'm so glad you made it," the nurse says. "He's just about ready to go."

On to the big hospital, Ellie knows, and realizes that this must be the woman who called her. She is young, even younger than Ellie, even shorter, with straight, brown hair pulled tightly back, a soft-looking round face and round, blue eyes. She had sounded so comfortingly unofficial on the phone, timid, apologetic almost, clearly not savoring the job, like she'd been the one to draw the shortest straw. A broken leg, she'd said at first. Multiple trauma, she'd said second, and to hurry and try to get there before he was transferred.

The nurse turns back into the room and yells so loudly it's confusing to Ellie, as loud as she'd yell were she trying to communicate with someone far outside the room. "Mr. Babineau. You're wife's here." And then to Ellie she says in a normal voice, "He's been asking for you."

And at these words, Ellie feels a little rush of surprise, that he has, considering what he's been going through, thought to ask for her, has said her name aloud to all these people who do not know her. She understands suddenly that she is important here.

"That you, Little Cabbage?" he says.

She says, "Yes, Babineau. It's me," and moves quickly into the room toward his voice, the one thing that is familiar to her. But when she sees his face, it isn't. It is his face, but his face as she has never seen it. His mouth moving, talking and talking in the voice she knows, and coming from a face that would be his, were he dead.

three

Just a month or so before his fiftieth year, if you could see through Gerard Babineau, right to the bones of his body, you would see very little amiss. There is his delicate fibula, ghostlike white, sweeping from ankle to knee, posing like the foolhardy protector before the bigger, stronger tibia. Still, the tibia is a graceful and slender bone, a more solid white than the fibula, but smaller than the thick and sturdy femur, that takes us all the way up to the perfect hip and pelvis, and rests on the amazing complexity of the knee. So much depending on this hinge, created and connected by bone and ligaments, cartilage and nerves, so that the bones above and below, whole and strong as they are, can work at optimum efficiency. And in this man, Gerard Babineau, they are. No foreign objects to hold things together, no crooked shadows of past breaks healed.

Only one, the small bone on the right side of his right hand, broken about ten years before, in the dead of a New England winter, when finding his car would not start, he got out of it and hit the hood with the side of his closed fist as hard as he possibly could.

He was not really angry at his car. He liked the car, a little secondhand Nova that he'd bought from the owner of the town's Shell station. Usually, the car was pretty reliable. He was mad, really, at the errand he'd just completed: dropping off Christmas presents for his children at his children's house so they'd have more presents to open on the first Christmas morning he would not spend with them because he did not live with them in the sagging, gray asbestos-sided, broken-down-looking house they'd just moved into on this slummy treeless street in this stupid harbor town that he hated. Cutesy shops, in brick mill buildings, where children used to process fish, surrounded by streets like this one, that the tourists didn't see. Where his children lived with his crazy ex-wife who he still wanted to fuck everytime she dragged on one of the Pall Malls she still smoked.

After he rolled around in the slush and snow for a while, holding his hand with his other hand and cursing colorfully, he decided to get up, sweating now, and worried he might vomit, something he really didn't like doing at all, and get back in his car and try it again. This time it started, like it had just wanted to play a trick on him. Like the whole thing was a big joke. Like the car, whom he'd optimistically named Constance, had wanted to see just how far she could push him. Just like a fucking woman, he thought. Should have named it Butch. And then he pulled out, and drove with his left hand only, the twenty minutes home, to the filthy apartment he regretted having agreed to share with his friend and teaching colleague, Stephen Borger, who was also on his way to getting divorced and was an incredible slob, to the point where Babineau had started to feel some stirring of pity for the guy's wife.

But on this night, Babineau was glad he was there, so Borger could go out and get more beer for them than he knew was in the refrigerator, and some Jim Beam while he was at it, wanting to pour the stuff on his hand like cowboys did on bullet wounds, then down his throat, so he could pass out, which he might just do anyway, because it was not letting up. Seemed like more than a bruise to him; enough so, that by about two A.M. and out on the back steps to piss into the snow and garbage bags, he fell down again — more from the pain, than the booze—and thought if he didn't freeze to death out there, he'd better have Borger drive him to a doctor. That nice Italian doctor who lived in the big brick house with the pillars a few blocks up on Main Street and who'd given him a prescription for the only sleeping pills that had ever worked.

That was, thus far, in Gerard Babineau's life, the only bone broken. Though this is not to say nothing else happened to him, that he hadn't come close to death.

This occurred in a bar in Okinawa when, fighting with someone he never saw again, he fell down a flight of stairs, so drunk it wasn't the fall that hurt him. It was a big glass brick the size of a cinderblock at the bottom. Some ornamental thing that bordered a little pool and fountain. Looked like a big block of ice that his head hit hard enough to break into a number of pieces. His skull, however, didn't, though his scalp opened up big time and scared the shit out of his buddies. Lots of blood and glass, a piece of which they sewed right into him and which eased itself out some years later when he'd left the Corps and was sitting in the middle of a political philosophy class in graduate school, already the father of four kids, spaced, a year, a year, a year, and then three years apart.

And after the fall and the broken hand, there was, it's true, one more injury, more recent than the other two, and which he still felt. And still, though he'd kind of brought it on himself, he wasn't remorseful about the incident that caused it: punching out a friend turned college administrator–ex-friend. He was just sorry the injury had been misdiagnosed, that he'd believed the pompous mediocre orthopod at the rinky-dink hospital in the town next to his. A bad sprain, he'd said, but it had to have been something else, torn ligaments, something, because it never felt right again.

He'd had to give up running. So he'd taken up power walking, which he was afraid, at first, might be a pussy sport. He'd been running since the Marine Corps, since before it was a fad and everyone did it and power walking was a fad already, when he'd started to do it, too. He found it, though, to be a pretty good aerobic workout, especially when he carried two-pound dumbbells in his hands and did some repetitions after. And he wished Ellie would do it with him, but she said, how could she, with

Lithe and all, and she could get the same workout running for twenty minutes and she liked running, so she wouldn't do it with him. Only sometimes when one of his kids was around to watch Lithe; but then she'd slow his pace and talk too much, so it became more of a pussy walk than a power walk, so maybe it was just as well.

And still he cursed The Dean. The Fucking Dean he called him, refusing to call him by name again. The other buddy he'd had besides Borger, who he'd taught with, who he'd gotten drunk with one night at a bar up at the beach in New Hampshire. The crazy Greek who decided he wanted to steal some live lobsters from the famous eat-in-the-rough lobster pound up there, which put them both in jail for the night. The Fucking Dean who got married and bought himself a big house and a tractor mower and fucked up Babineau's ankle for him good. It was The Dean who'd made him bullshit enough to throw a punch and wrestle him down the carpeted suburban-house stairs, this time not landing on a glass brick, but on the side of his ankle, hard enough for them all, he and The Dean, and The Dean's screaming wife, to hear it go pop.

That too, was some years back, divorced from wife number two and married to wife number three, but at the time, with neither a mortgaged home, nor a tractor mower. Now the husband of Ellie Rifkin, and the recent father of child number five, and not many years after he and Ellie moved from the tiny attic apartment he'd had to find after he first met her. After the very first night he met her, in fact, when he'd returned home in the kind of light he remembered from sea duty that made the ocean and the sky the very same color of gray, and made him feel that he stood upon the only solid thing left in a world of no up or down or forward or back. For this reason, he did not like the beginning of day, or the beginning of night, and so he was driving well past the suburban street speed limit just to get inside, even if he was to be greeted by wife number two's interrogation, fore-drawn conclusions, and, he had to admit, legitimate rage. But just when he'd begun to brake for the turn onto college property, he saw his snare drum out on the curb.

He thought maybe it was an alcohol-induced hallucination, and that the time had come to finally give up the booze when he saw his black weight bench too, and on top of it a mound of his clothes, his framed photographs of jazz greats, his pipe stand, humidor, baseball mug, and the line-drive ball he'd fought off six kids to retrieve from under the seats of section B on opening day in 1974. Just about everything that was in the one room he said he was allowed to fart in, in that college-owned house, out there on the curb like the preliminary preparation for a whopper of a yard sale.

He got out of his car and watched a big red leaf wander downward from the maple tree above and land square in the center of the drum, as if the drum had provided it a target. Then he watched another land on his dusky pink and, according to his children, second most putrid polyester shirt beside the one he was at that moment wearing. She hadn't included his barbells and plates, books or records. Probably too heavy for her to carry, too strenuous for a woman who moved only when her long, skinny, brown cigarettes were out of reach.

From the day he'd done it, he couldn't figure out why he'd married her. Maybe it was something in the boudin blanc, he said, because he'd gone down to Lake Charles to visit his mother and there was Carly Thibodeau, wet-eyed, waiflike. They practically shared the same name, though he kept forgetting it was really McDonough, not the name she'd had when he'd last seen her, in high school, but the name of her very recently dead husband. Maybe that was it. Maybe widows turned him on and Borger's dirty socks didn't. Maybe it was that he saw her son, Trevor, was going to turn into a fruit if he didn't do something about it, and maybe he wanted to live in a civilized manner again and knew this was most easily accomplished by cohabitation with a representative of the opposite sex.

"But why?" he would say, "Why did she marry me? If she wasn't half-cocked, too? Maybe we were compatible after all," he would say. "Compatibly off our rockers." This examination of marriage number two, often undertaken while leaning on the lacquered wooden bar of his local tavern called Holiday's.

It had also been called McCales and DiAngelo's, but the red naugahyde booth couches, dark stained woodwork, the windmill-shaped Heineken clock, and the working-man clientele who called him The Professor had remained unchanged, as had the bar's proximity to him. Always it had been within walking distance of all the places he'd lived: the apartment with Borger, the college-owned house with wife number two, and the little attic apartment the college had also provided for him, but not without some delay, during which he lived on the other side of town in the house of wife number one.

She lived then with his four children, all in their teens now and was still, in his estimation, a buddy, a precarious buddy to be sure, but the person you made babies with, he contested, was about as permanently in your life as the babies you made. You could be friendly, or unfriendly, he figured, and friendly really was better for everyone, all told. Anyway, they had a long history. She was born and raised in the same state, she dated him in high school, dated him while he went to college, married him when she got pregnant, and left with him for Quantico, Puget Sound, then the Midwest, then New England, dropping babies all along the way, good Catholic that he was and that she'd converted into being. And now here she was, the path having last led her from the Harbor Town Slum to a big rented house in his town.

So for a short period that followed his early morning discovery of wife number two's makeshift, curbside dump, he lived in the home of wife number one. And because it was located far outside walking distance of his local tavern, and wanting, when he could, to be responsible about driving drunk, he chose to spend his evenings in his oldest son's third-floor room, standing the way he did when he lectured, leaning against the wall like it was a blackboard, one ankle crossed over the other, a thumb hooked into his belt, but in his free hand a bottle of beer; before him, his son grown recently handsome and well built, sitting on the floor in that impossible lotus position, the both of them talking pussy and politics well into the night and on into the first hours of the next day, and pissing into their empties when they felt the frequent urge.

Babineau couldn't have been more happy then. Marriage number two's misery concluded with neither his consent nor initiation, which considerably reduced his guilt, sheltered by wife number one who still smoked those Pall Malls, made great seafood gumbo, shrimp étouffé and jalapeño cornbread, with the added bonus of his son's nightly companionship, while he could anticipate the sweet pleasure provided by the company of that serious, earnest, and charmingly obliviously sensual college girl who lived in a town not so far south as to be inconvenient to reach. He couldn't really have had it any better, considering the fact that his domestic life had once again fallen apart, this time at the age of forty-one.

And each night he would wait contentedly for the beer and sleeping pills to do their combination and land him flat on his back on the mold-infested mattress that clogged his deviated septum, and snore and sleep as close as he could to the time that the rest of the world did it.

Ah, to be like the rest of the world. How he longed for this, how he loathed his own longing. "Sheep! Sheep! Baa! Baa!" he'd yell, leaning on the bar. And then, as eloquent and convincing and outrageous as he was when he wrote his column, essays, radio commentaries; famously indifferent to the sensibilities of any audience he addressed in any forum, he would expound, spewing words like sparks from a welder's torch, his audience entranced by the danger and the dazzle.

He was all power then, and he would do anything to prolong

what he was. This was best accomplished, he found, with beer followed by Metaxa, or beer followed by bourbon. So that when the lights flashed on and mercilessly stayed on to the announcement of *Closing, Closing, Closing,* bellowed by the bartender like the name of a station stop at the end of a train run, he could leave. He could open the door, and step out into the late night motionlessness of the main street of his town and walk home under the big dark sky he felt hanging there just above the streetlights, like a warehouse roof built with an undetected structural flaw. So he could walk home beneath it and not have to remember doing so the next day, or remember opening the door to all his various homes, and how his feet hissed on their worn kitchen linoleum, loud enough in that quiet to make his teeth grit, the one with Borger, the one with wife number two, and the little attic apartment he'd lived in briefly by himself until Ellie Rifkin wanted to live in it with him.

He couldn't say no. "Hell," he said, "we were stuck together four days straight during the blizzard, nothing to eat but canned peas and saltines and we didn't have one fight." And you wouldn't see those slimy textured, fat and heavy fashion magazines that cluttered the tops of toilet tanks, couches, and bedside tables in the home of marriage number two in Ellie Rifkin's hands. Just books. No *Vogue,* no *Cosmopolitan* with their harebrained articles on how to prevent wrinkles and cellulite and fat and all the things Ellie didn't have to worry about yet. But still, he would have sworn to Mother Mary that she was twenty-seven the night he'd first met her.

The way she drank that rotgut Gallo wine as if it were some fine Chardonnay, the little aristocratic pinky poking up. He knew right then she came from money. The way she picked the shells from the Bucket O' Shrimp they'd agreed to share with nails she didn't waste her life painting.

"Hey, you're hogging," he'd said. "I thought we were sharing."

"We are," she said, jerking back her hand. Serious, worried that she might have, in fact, unwittingly taken more than she should have.

It was endearing. And more so when he saw her realize that he was teasing, and smile and go for more.

That face, those lips. She had to be older than the rest of the table, the kind who takes a few years off and returns committed and hardworking. His favorite kind of student to teach. "You've got a smoker's mouth," he said, and offered her his pack.

She glanced at it, then looked up and across the table, and leaned forward like she was trying to hear the conversation on the other side, but the table was big and round, and, seeming to give up, she looked back at him to see he hadn't moved, the pack still extended. She laughed suddenly and said, "Oh, me. No, I don't smoke."

"You're putting me on," he said. He was astonished.

"No. Really," she said, "I hate cigarettes."

"But that mouth," he said. "You mean to tell me that mouth has not ever taken a drag from a cigarette?"

"Never," she said. "Sorry." She smiled and picked up another shrimp.

But he continued to look at her. He simply could not be wrong. He was never wrong about this. He took for himself the cigarette he'd intended for her, and still keeping his eyes on her, felt in his shirt pocket for his silver Zippo lighter. He lit the cigarette and blew the smoke to the side without turning his face, just twisting his mouth to do it. She was a smoker. There was no doubt about it. He never made that mistake. She was a smoker who just didn't know she was. That was it. Solved. And he said, "Before you're finished knowing me, you'll be hooked. Addicted. You," he said and pointed a finger at her.

"Oh?" she said. She was looking down at the shrimp she was peeling. Then raising just her eyes she said, "And when will I be finished knowing you?"

He smiled, hoping smoothly, because her sudden boldness scared him a little. And he hoped the smile had implied a kiss, sometime pretty soon and out of sight of the other classmates at the restaurant table, and their professor who had invited him, even gotten his department to pay some relatively good money for the lecture Babineau had delivered that afternoon. He said to her, "Maybe tonight. Maybe tomorrow. Maybe after a short and stormy marriage 'cause I'm just an old fart and you've got places to go."

"Well then," she said, "You'll have to work fast."

The kiss, accomplished in the privacy provided by the hallway leading to the restaurant bathrooms, was not exactly what he'd expected. She'd practically gagged him with her tongue. A little eager beaver, he thought. And then he thought maybe he should really find out just how old she was. So he asked her. And she told him, and he reeled back into the smelly hallway, staggered, like he'd just taken a punch, and said, "Nine-fucking teen! Nine-fucking-teen! I am doomed."

four

She thinks she is lost. And she'd listened so carefully, too. Had even copied over the directions while she'd waited for his son to arrive. But she has been driving now for what feels like too long on a windy rural road, searching for the clinic that she could have passed, that could still be ahead, that could be on another road altogether. And her progress impeded, the possibility of a delay caused by something she cannot immediately fix or figure out, she feels her will gigantic, push and rise and expand and crest, and she begins to moan.

As she has already this night, sitting at the edge of her bed. Rocking. Her cold hands pressed between her thighs, her whole body gone cold and shaky, waiting and waiting for Corey.

"He has the car," she says to him, the closest living family member, and about as dependable as the dilapidated tank of a car he drives. "I need your car," she says. "Now. Yes. Yes. A broken leg they said," she says and stops there because it is impossible for her to say the other thing, the second thing the woman on the phone has said. That later makes her know with a calm fatalistic clarity that the blue lights on the other side of the highway, six cruiser's worth at least, are his.

The dog stands in front of her, sniffs at the handle of the sliding glass door, fool that he is. Fool. Fool. Stupid dog. His oblivion both enviable and loathsome. Well, no one can boast about the acuity of golden retrievers.

She puts her hands over her face. And not intending to speak, she says, "Where is he? Where is he?" Then pushes her hands, palms pressed, back between her thighs, rocks forward, and moans again. The dog wags his tail. Stops wagging his tail, and looks at her.

She hears her daughter shift and sigh. She sleeps behind her in the center of the bed where she ends up just about every night, having come back and back again from the very first time Ellie let her in. Ellie clamps her lips together and puts her hands over her face again, the blindness they make somehow better, like it is doing to her, what it does to horses to get them to run from a burning barn. Lithe should not be awakened. She already has been, by the phone, the light turned on, shut off, dresser drawers pulled out and shoved in. And has heard her mother say to her that Daddy was in an accident, but he'll be okay. Mommy has to go to him, but Corey will stay with you. How she likes Corey. How Corey is funny. And Lithe had laid back down and watched, until she slept again.

Ellie should not, must not wake her. And she should not make things worse for the one inside of her, must not add wailing and keening to what surely is already a terrible din of heartbeat and the propulsion of blood and air. No escape for the little stranger, as she thinks of it. Poor thing. Poor thing. Stuck with her right to the end.

She puts her hands on her belly and can feel the cold from them through her clothing. And waits. And waits. The dog walks from the door to her feet, drops into a curl, puts his chin on his paws, and sighs. And still she waits until she is sure Corey has fallen back to sleep. He must have fallen back to sleep. Typical. So typical. And is up then, tripping over the dog and punching numbers, hoping she remembers them right, ready to scream at him. Scream, even if she does wake Lithe, when she sees headlights hit the glass door and hears the dog growl.

The road is so dark. Not a house. Nothing. She wonders if maybe it was a left off the exit. Maybe she passed it. She must have passed it. Or maybe it is around the next bend in the road; but it isn't. Woods and more woods and she says, Please. Please. Please. And does not want to think about who it is she has addressed. Exactly who she is begging.

Babineau is the one who speaks to God, lying next to her in bed, when they do occasionally go there at the same time, so silently she does not know, and interrupts him with conversation or a touch, and he raises a finger, like he is holding his breath to outwit an attack of hiccups, until he's done. That is how he prays.

It is Babineau who can see ghosts, who has been slain, who wears the plain silver cross that hits her nose and mouth until she catches it between her teeth, releases when he is done. And it's Babineau who believes that what he receives every Sunday, and lately each weekday morning, too, is truly Christ's body and His blood.

And here, now she is praying. Religious at her own convenience. Hypocrite. Only when she really wants something, like to see a Goddamn sign for the Goddamn Emergency Medical Clinic that seems to have been built so far from civilization that those seeking its services are sure to be dead on arrival.

Then there it is. A white cube, lit from the inside, glowing out of the dark like something dropped from outer space, proclaiming in big blue block letters, the name of her first destination.

five

Fucked a Jewish girl in that town," he said when he heard where she lived. "Only Jewish girl I ever fucked. Her name was Ruthie Schwartz." And then she told him she was Jewish, too. Amazing coincidence. Amazing period. 'Cause he could have sworn she was a rich WASP, the blond hair, the blue, maybe green eyes, the Anglo Saxon jawline. Like his students. Still, he bet she drove a Volvo and told her so on the way out of the restaurant.

"Wrong again," she said.

It was a Rabbit, and man she drove it fast. He wondered if she meant to lose him, but she seemed happy enough when he'd pulled up, parked behind her, worried the old emergency brake might slip on this steep hill of a street she lived on. She waited for him on the porch, smiling, and didn't move until he stood right in front of her, thought now he should kiss her, when she kind of whirled and unlocked the door and started up the stairs, and more stairs and more, and by the last flight he wasn't looking at her ass anymore. Just trying to breathe so she wouldn't hear it, said, "Jesus Christ. You carry groceries up this shit every day?"

She turned and looked down at him, and with a quick, cocky smile said, "Not every day."

"Apparently, no days at all," he said when he'd walked the long railroad hall straight back to the refrigerator in search of beer.

"What?" she said.

"What the hell do y'all eat here?" he said. "Tofu? A little brown rice?"

"We eat," she said.

"No beer," he said. And turned to see she was holding a bottle of cheap, dry sherry.

"This is it," she said.

They sat on her couch in her living room in the dark. She put on music, a male singer with a sickly sweet voice that he heard sometimes when he was searching for the baseball scores. And all he could think about was how he would never get it up. He knew. Never under these circumstances which were not unfamiliar.

There'd been his student, Hilary, who he couldn't help but think of. And the other student who he'd already thought of, Ruthie Schwartz. But she was mean. He couldn't figure out if this girl was mean or not. Kind of like Ruthie, and kind of like Hilary, too. And he had loved Hilary. Who'd been his girlfriend between wife number one and wife number two. And she had broken his heart; giving him the first opportunity he'd had to execute his recipe for heartbreak cure, which entailed listening to Bob Dylan, drunk for three days, while taking mental note of every single bad thing about her, right down to the outy mole on the underside of her left tit, which really had never bothered him when she loved him, but he'd decided, once she didn't anymore, that it should have.

Purged. He'd purged her from him, and had passed the recipe on to Borger and others. Good ol' Dylan.

They were kissing. On a couch that maybe was a bed made to look like a couch. It was too high, too wide, and it creaked. If he leaned in search of support, he'd practically be lying down. If he boosted himself, to move closer to the wall and pillows, his feet might dangle. He ran his tongue over the sharp edges of her top teeth and hoped the crunches he did every morning would prevent his straining lower back from going out. He wiggled his tongue around in her mouth. They needed some suction. They needed to swallow. He opened his mouth wider. She bit his lower lip. Nothing. *Nada.* Dead as a two-day-old fish.

"You know," he said into her mouth, then pulled away, stretching strings of saliva between them. She smiled, embarrassed. They both wiped their mouths. "No way am I going to get it up tonight. The booze," he said, though he knew he wasn't really that drunk.

She smiled, a generous smile. Not patronizing or scornful, as he'd feared. "Probably, it's best," she said.

"But it doesn't mean," he said, "that we have to stay here on this fucking weird little couch of yours."

She laughed and got up. She took his hand and led him down the hall, back to the kitchen, into her room which was just off of it, next to the closed door of another room with light shining from the bottom crack, that she said was her roommate Jane's. "Jane's fine," she said, though he hadn't been particularly worried about Jane.

And once in her room, he couldn't believe how fast she was out of her clothes and in her bed, so that she was just lying there, watching him in the light from the street, pulling down his pants. He turned away from her and stood in the corner farthest from the bed, felt his gut push against the front of his shorts, his love-handles at the sides, felt the whole, lumpy distortion of a body that had once weighed a puny 105 pounds when he'd got his driver's license in downtown Lake Charles, and the body he had pumped up into something he at times couldn't recognize. He said to her, "Don't ever think that this situation, you know, the older man, younger girl, I mean, woman, thing makes me feel like some kind of stud. Okay? Don't believe that shit." And he stopped. He stood still with his pants at his ankles, his socks still on, his shirt unbuttoned, his boxers hanging off his non-ass, and he looked at the wall and sighed, thinking, What the fuck. What the fuck am I doing here? Until he heard her voice. Until he heard it say, "Babineau. Babineau. It's all right. Come to bed."

Which he did. Where they lay naked and drank sherry from big goblets and sang. She had an amazing voice, a beautiful voice, strong and sure, a real pro's and sang with it sad pop songs that he knew, all right, but would never choose to go out and buy. He sang her Sinatra, the way Sinatra would sing it, and she laughed, but he wasn't trying to be funny. In fact he thought he'd done a damn good job on "Under My Skin," so before she could sing another one, he started in on "Lush Life" and sang the whole thing, every last word, just to show her. And watched her suffer a little. Because of course the song was too long for even a prolonged smile. So she had to give it a rest. She sipped her sherry. Dipped her eyes to her wristwatch. But she was being polite. Definitely polite. Well, we all can't be Joan Baez, Carly Simon types. But at least he didn't sing fluff. He sang the classics. Billy Strayhorn, "who wrote that song when he was sixteen. Sixteen. For the Duke," he said to her. "And it bored you."

"No," she said, startled, her head lifting fast from the pillow. "It didn't bore me."

He looked at her.

"It didn't. It was good. You were good. I mean it's a hard one without music. Sing another one."

"Nah," he said. "No more."

"Oh, come on," she said. "I really didn't mean to hurt your feelings."

"Well," he said, and smiled, lying on his back and looking at the glass he held clamped to the center of his chest like a suction arrow, "you did."

"Oh come on, Babineau," she said. "Please? Just sing one more."

"If you insist," he said. And sang "Funny Valentine," not quite sure what note he'd ended up on when he got to the word *stay,* because the one he was supposed to hit was too high, and he watched her while he sang whatever came to mind, along with the notes that followed it. And he had to admit she tried hard. She was a good sport. Anyone else would have said he couldn't sing for shit. And they'd be right, of course.

When he was done, he lit a cigarette, took the first drag, and offered the next one to her, holding the filter toward her between his index and middle fingers, so she could more easily lift it out.

"No thanks," she said. "Really. No."

"Come on. Just a drag. You don't even have to inhale."

"No. Really," she said.

"Oh, Eleanor. Those beautiful lips. That smoker's mouth. One drag. Just one. Do it, Ellie. For me."

She leaned forward, her face resigned, stoic, not too sexy, he had to admit, and took a pull, right from where it was, and straightened, watching him watching her, while she held the smoke in her mouth for a moment, approximating the time of inhalation, and then released it, slowly.

"Jesus," he said. "That was a beautiful sight," and closed his eyes and lay back on the pillow to draw a deep breath. "Whew," he said, opened his eyes again, and then took a drag himself. "I do believe you momentarily did stir Peter Pecker from his deep slumber."

She laughed. She was looking into his eyes. Green eyes. She had green eyes.

"You're one beautiful woman," he said to her. And there was the big broad smile. Lots of good straight teeth. She was hooked.

six

The rooms change. The bed does not. And there is that human characteristic. That anthropological phenomenon, if you will. The human claim to habitat by way of adornment. The body, yes, draped with clothing, hung with jewelry and sculpted hair. And the place the body resides. In this case Babineau's bed. Chosen quickly, randomly as it must have been on that first night, out of all those others just like it, generic, functional, ugly. It transforms.

The longer he lies in it, the more there is that dangles from it, is stuck onto it. The raised horizontal bar that functions officially to support the clothesline rope and four black weights, the metal triangle he must grip to pull on during sheet changing and bedpan insertion, supports as well a blue-and-black ceramic evil eye, a leather medicine pouch, a pipe-cleaner mobile made by the daughter, Lithe. And cards depicting color photographs of open places, usually at sunset. All brought by friends, sent to them by strangers.

She thinks they should add the bent quarter.

"Drill a hole in it. Thread it with rawhide," he said, roused early on, when she first showed it to him, from his morphine-driven vigil. Both of them finding in it a perverse fascination. Laid upon a flat surface, it wobbled. Good enough to pass for some kind of artifact or fetish displayed under glass, folk stories abounding about the one who bent it barehanded.

A Honda, though, they knew, had been the culprit. And she could not hang it from her neck as he'd suggested, or the bed, like a gargoyle, scaring evil with evil, because the lawyer grabbed it for evidence and manipulated it all around in his hands and between his fingers where he sat across his desk from her. It was that kind of object. Its shape and density seductive. Asking to be touched. Like a shark's tooth.

seven

His skin felt thick to her, like it would resist the penetration of anything sharp. And as she kissed it, touched it, licked it, she wondered if he felt this as something far off; dulled, the way the taste of food can be by illness. The room was quiet enough for her to hear the sounds her mouth made, the crack of her joints. She noticed, because with him, silence was unusual. Already she knew he did not like it, from the way he talked more rapidly, more cleverly, when he felt it threaten.

They lay on her living room floor, blue and green Indian print pillows surrounding, not beneath them. Too small and springy, they'd squeezed right out from under their weight. So they lay directly on the hard wood and in the sun because she'd said how she loved the way the sun made the wood warm, her skin so warm and the fall chill right on the other side of the long bay windows. She'd gone to sit in it, and he'd joined her, and now this was what was happening.

It had not been her plan. She really ought to be writing a paper for Evolution on camouflage and deceptive coloring. That was what she would have been doing if she hadn't driven up, home from her eight A.M. class, to see him sitting on her front stoop, smoking a pipe, the tobacco taste still in his mouth, the smell of it in his beard.

He'd said to her, "Where you been?" and that he'd been freezing his *cajones* off waiting for her, and she thought for a moment that she must have forgotten something.

"Sorry," she said, "I was just talking to some people. If I'd known you were here . . . ," she said, but felt bad, particularly about how cold he was. He'd actually suffered to see her, and she wanted to make it up to him. "Want some tea? I'll make you some hot tea," she said, unlocking the door and thinking of how long this unexpected visit might take, which would require her to reorganize her day, the time she'd allotted for her paper, for her workout, for lunch, that all would have been accomplished in time to get to her afternoon class.

She sat astride him, down to her underpants and the undershirt she preferred to bras. She leaned down, kissed his shoulder, and looked through her hair at her watch. Forget the paper for today. It would have to wait, and never one to leave things to the last minute, she could do it tomorrow. That's what she'd do. And she really should loosen up a little. Here she was, after all, making love on a Wednesday morning, on her living room floor like a real free spirit. She should go with it, experience it. Give in. The way she had the week before, to him and the wine and his request to go home with her. Life was there to live, after all. This was her philosophy.

He was hairy. He was bearish. It wasn't unpleasant, exactly. It wasn't like the man she had loved, either. He'd been tall, smooth skinned, soft skinned, all the steep grades, flat plains, knobby summits of the male anatomy revealed. She had loved him, not so long ago. She had been the one to sit on his stoop when she knew he wasn't there, and might not even be coming.

Babineau lifted the bottom of her undershirt. She did not really want to take it off, but she raised her arms, and leaned forward to help him, simply because compliance was easier than resistance. She straightened, shook back her hair, and heard him say, "Mmmm."

This was about her breasts, she knew. Small, not particularly shapely, but at such a moment men never seemed to be picky. His hands were on them now, and she knew her nipples were hardening at the touch and that he'd think this was a manifestation of her pleasure. But it was just a response. Not much different from the quick retraction, she'd seen in an Evolution film, of the sea anemone's tentacles at the most benign stimulation. Her breasts could just as well have done that, were they able. But this way, they could fool. And she was glad because she really couldn't stop things now.

She'd be a cocktease if she did. And she should know: kissing always led to this. But to have stopped him from kissing her would have been so dramatic, such an overreaction. Just a kiss, after all. She didn't want him to think she was frigid or something. Same, if she'd not invited him up. After all, he'd come to surprise her, had waited for her in the cold. It would have been mean to send him away. And she liked him. It wasn't like she didn't like him. Though he wasn't exactly her type. Far from it, in fact, with those cowboy boots that poked so oddly from the wide bottoms of his chino pants, and his polyester, of all things, loud print shirts. And his age. It wasn't like she had a father complex and deliberately pursued older and married, well, separated, it was true, men. But he was funny. Not dull, that was for sure. And he was accomplished. Well known. He was on the radio sometimes. He'd written her class text. And out of the six other women who'd been sitting at that restaurant table, he'd chosen her.

Now, he was inside her. Panties off, diaphragm in place, it wouldn't be long. It wasn't very complicated. Only problem was the floor against her knees. It was very hard, like it had gotten harder and was not the same floor she'd first gone to sit on in the sun. Smooth and warm then, now against her kneecaps it felt as unforgiving as marble. And the sun had turned hot. She could smell her own body, hoped he couldn't, and wished she could stop and climb off to rub her knees and catch her breath. So she moved faster, concentrated, the way she did when she faltered on a long, hard run, resolving just to get it finished.

And did, finally, thank God, able to sit back, remove the weight from her knees, and watch his face and listen to his sounds while she waited for the appropriate time to remove herself from him and lie down and rest.

But then he was laughing. His whole body was jerking beneath hers, and she smiled, uncertain, preparing to be teased for something ridiculous that she didn't know she'd done. Then realizing: it wasn't laughing he was doing. And after a big, open-mouthed gasp, he was weeping audibly, sobs, that sounded as close to boo hoo as she'd ever heard.

She did not move, did not speak, still looking, still unsure whether she should believe he was really doing what she saw he was, until there was no mistaking it. And then she was repelled, embarrassed, and appalled by her own heartlessness. Naturally she should ask him what was wrong? What was it? The questions alone conveying sympathy. But she didn't want to know the answer, was too afraid he'd really tell her. And as he continued to weep, and would not stop, or even cover his face, she felt her body stiffen, dry like clay, and her stomach turn, as she recognized, and grew more certain, more certain, that she was a part of the cause. That she hadn't fooled him for a second, that he knew, and had known all along, and had chosen to simply bear her indifference, uncomplaining, until he couldn't anymore, until it, along with all the things she didn't want to know about, had combined to make him feel something worse she knew, than the worst kind of loneliness.

So she sat there, still astride him, naked, knees aching, plain as day, mouth shut and stock still, with no other choice for defense, but immobility and silence.

eight

"You should hear this girl sing," he told Borger.

They stood at the corner of the bar nearest the door. Their usual place, at their usual time, when most of the barroom had emptied of the after-work happy-hour drinkers, because they had dinner waiting, "Leaving us for 'loser hour,'" Babineau would say. "For the poor fuckers who can't keep a woman." But he liked it. He liked the laboratory look of the gallon glass jar full of clear vinegar and the firm white eggs that he made his dinner. He liked the near-empty bar, dark before the two high and tiny windows showed it was outside, the TV off because no one was watching it, the radio turned low, and himself at the start of what he predicted would be one of those good, contemplative drunks.

Though Borger was getting on his nerves with his skepticism and his height. Borger, so tall he could put the flat of his palm on Babineau's forehead, arm extended, and Babineau would be swinging at air. Already though, the beer was dulling the edge, and pretty soon the bourbon that sat neat, and as yet untouched beside it, would send him off the deck.

That's how he thought of it, what it felt like. The jets he'd watched from the conning tower, the way that big mother of a ship kind of spit them up into the air. Literally no room for error, or else you'd end up like that one pilot, whose plane just skittered and fell off the end. And the pilot, quick enough, but not high enough to eject, was slapped silly by the water's surface and lay there on it, facedown, for the few seconds the sailors had, to run around like crazy, doing their drill for real, before the parachute got full enough with ocean to pull him under and down. Gone. So damn fast, Babineau couldn't really blame the fucked-upness of the Navy that time. Like when his drunks went the same way. He knew he had only himself to blame.

"Babineau's back to cradle robbing," Borger said to the bartender, Bryan, who stood at the center of the bar washing glasses. "This time she can sing. So what's she sing, Bab? 'Twinkle, Twinkle'?"

"He just wants some," Babineau said.

"Damn right," Borger said.

The bartender smiled without looking up from his dunk, dunk, in the rack rhythm. Babineau liked him, admired him, a feisty boy from a big Irish family, working his way through law school. Got his fiancée all ready and waiting, cute squeaky-clean girl that she was. Babineau watched the flex of his biceps and triceps as the bartender lifted and submerged the glasses, noticed how the muscles pulled tight the short sleeve of his white Izod-type shirt, then tapered to his elbow. Babineau couldn't get that definition, try as he might, or the forearm veins. He wanted those veins, but all he got was bulk. He said, "Don't listen to him, Bryan. She might be young, but she's old."

"Oh, yeah," said Borger. "That makes perfect sense. But could you perhaps elaborate for us, Babble, I mean, Babby. Bryan here, almost-attorney-at-law, might need more evidence to prosecute you for statu-horniness."

"Funny," Babineau said.

"I prefer to think of myself as witty, thank you. Quick-witted." He pushed his glasses up to the bridge of his nose and poured more beer into his glass, but didn't drink any.

Babineau looked at the head settle. "There's something about her," and thought, What? A remoteness. Like she'd lived a couple of lives before this one and something of the people she'd been lay down deep in the person she was now. Out of his reach, just out of his reach. It was tantalizing. It was infuriating. And he didn't even believe in that multiple life shit.

It was past time for him to speak again so he said, "She's serious. It's sexy. What can I say?"

"Innocent, maybe? Unspoiled? Pure? Childlike, perhaps?"

"Hey. She's no virgin, Borger, if that's what you're after."

"Well, certainly not after making your acquaintance, I'm sure," said Borger. He took a swallow of beer. "So when am I going to meet her?"

"You say she sings?" Bryan said, now holding a rag, and wiping the inside of a thick glass ashtray.

"Yeah," Babineau said. "You know, Carly Simon, Carole King kind of stuff."

"Have her come sing."

"Here?"

"No. DJs. They got live music there."

"Yeah, yeah. That's right. Some of my students play there. Morgan. You know Morgan," he said to Borger. "My African tribesman from Ghana. Calls me Professor Boppy-no. You had him. I'll talk to him. He can arrange it."

"You think she'll do it?" Borger said.

"She'll do it. She's not shy. She knows she's good," only discovering he knew this by saying it, and not sure he liked it. Humility certainly a more attractive quality than pride. But alluring. Definitely alluring, that kind of cockiness. "Morgan and I will make it happen," he said. "Good thinking, Bryan," he said, excited by the prospect. He'd always thought people looked most beautiful when they sang, like it gave mortals a living glimpse of the angels he believed they would all become.

He switched his cigarette from his right to his left hand, to take up his bourbon, a generous shot, shining both dark and light amber in the thick, faceted glass, then placed it to his lips, knocked it back, wiped his mouth, exhaled with a gasp, and said, "Shitfire, Borger," for no real reason but to celebrate the goodness of how it felt going down.

And this is when she falls in love with him; the whole bar hooting and stomping because she has surprised them by not sounding the way her long blond hair and makeup-less face made them think she would. And walking triumphant, off the parquet and out of the lights, she sees she has surprised him, too. That though he smiles and stretches toward her the arm that will publicly claim her, his eyes are afraid. They are afraid and full of yearning, like the eyes of a child who has no choice but to ask for tenderness from the same hand that beats him. And it breaks her heart.

nine

They say he's got some circulation to his toes. It's the first she's heard that there may be some question of this and it makes her wonder, really what is left of him between him and the clean pale feet she's been watching them poke and observe. Her image changes now from cracked white bones to red, just a mess of red. Not so much different from what her daughter will draw when Ellie asks her to draw what she thinks of when she thinks of what happened to him.

But from the beginning everything has been so clean. It's hard to believe. Here again, in another examining room off of Emergency in the big hospital, the sheets that cover him are crisp and white, the only injury visible to her are the scrapes on his forearms that are not much different from what he might have gotten falling off a bike.

But now he is beginning to suffer. His back. His back hurts, he says. And tries to lift himself to reach behind, but can't. The complaint is a puzzling one, since as far as she's been told, his legs, not his back, would be what would hurt, if anything were to. And she sees the young doctor is also puzzled and concerned and immediately begins to ask him questions because his back had not been considered, until then, to be imperiled. And it isn't, really, they find out. Compressed fractures that you can't do much for, determined from one of the pictures she'd waited and waited in a waiting room for them to take, and now waits with him for them to develop. Then they will knock him out.

Which is what he is begging them to do. He says, "Knock me out. Knock me out. Please." And says to her. "Tell them, Little Cabbage, to knock me out."

She tells them. But they can't. Not until all the pictures are back and they've made a thorough assessment of his condition. And she tells him. And he says, "Well tell them to hurry up. Tell them to hurry up. Please." And turns his face away from her and turns it back to her and away and says, "Oh shit. Oh shit. Oh shit."

"Soon, Babineau." She keeps saying, "Soon," to him and to herself as well. Because she's not sure she can bear much longer the watching of his anguish that she cannot relieve. The way he keeps trying to touch his back and can't. It is doing something to her. Something like what exposure to high-voltage power lines might do, or some extreme magnetic field. It pulls at her insides, makes it hard for her to breathe, makes her stomach turn, her face hot, her knees unreliable. She wonders if there's a danger of her miscarrying, wonders if maybe she should tell someone about her being pregnant. But the very thought of directing anyone's attention away from his needs, so much graver than hers, is offensive to her, shameful. And thinks, anyway, women only lose babies from this kind of thing in movies. Wimpy women. Vomiting, though, is a different matter, something that is becoming a real possibility, along with fainting. But that's another thing pregnant women only do in movies, and because she has never fainted in her life, she's not really sure that's what it is she thinks she feels like she might do.

Still, she stands beside him, and has not stopped talking to him, wanting her voice and the things she makes it say to calm them both, but it seems as ineffectual as her touch, her hand on his wrist. That it feels like his wrist as his wrist has always felt, makes her a little less afraid, but clearly, the feel of her hand on it is doing nothing for him. He is begging her and begging her to make them give him something. "Jesus. Jesus. Jesus," he says turning and turning his head from side to side. She is sure her heart and her lungs are pulling right out of her body. Then she jerks forward, gagging, and only then, when it's not a decision anymore does she go.

Past a nurse who is saying something to her, and out the open door of the examining room, hand pressed to her mouth, and down the hall to the bathroom she'd gone to hours ago during the waiting-room wait, pushing the door just as she had then, the wrong way, pulling it outward, the right way, striding headlong to the farther of the two mercifully empty stalls and stopping herself as she would in a fall, arms outstretched, taking her full weight, until she drops to her knees, gagging and spitting and heaving, and heaving again, absolutely nothing into the glassy and undisturbed water.

You'd think she would have known. That she would have been awakened, not by a telephone, but by a vision: Babineau flying. Just as she was told months later on a visit to their home by the same state trooper she spoke to that first night. "Up and over the car, and he lands right here," he says pointing to the narrow trunk of the sporty little Honda a single, young woman would be inclined to buy for herself. Blood spills over the edge and onto and over the bumper, and in the glossy 8-x-10 black-and-white investigative photo it looks like oil. The same thick black as the pool that spreads from beneath the driver's door of the dented Pinto in a picture she holds behind the one she's looking at now. The pool he thought was blood was oil. Blood and oil. Oil and blood. Under one car it's oil, on another it's blood. His.

Babineau declines a look, but she has insisted upon seeing it, demands not some, but all of the photos be handed over by the reluctant trooper. She wants to see for real what she could only imagine over and over again for all these months past. And finds out he was not on the ground after all, and, as the state trooper tells it, landed on his back, and lay there, wondering what the hell happened, and asking what the hell he was looking at, which turned out to be big, green lit-up letters affixed to the side of an industrial park building that spelled the name of a computer company.

Accuracy was the key. It made her as close to being there as she could get. With him, as she had so wanted to be, as she still longs to have been. Running to him, running to him to tell him he would be all right, to cradle his head in her arms, and tell him she was there, she was there and he should not be afraid.

You would have thought, if not a vision, at least a premonition, a sense of dread or doom. But she'd gone to bed happy that night. And awakened slowly to ringing, a ringing. Until she identified the sound to be that of a phone. Until she thought a ringing phone is a thing that is answered. Until she realized it was she who must answer it. But by then it was too late. Awake now, she lay listening to the machine down the hall go through its motions, his voice telling the caller whose home they'd reached and what they should do to leave a message. Then Sara Vaughn and the clicking of the machine shutting itself off. So all she could do was lie there, eyes open, heart fast beating, wondering if it had been him, or if it had been someone else. Waiting, and hoping for it to ring again because this time she'd be able to find out.

ten

He couldn't believe how much shit she had. Why do women have so much shit, he thought, and chain-smoked unabashedly as he watched the movers bring it in. Same thing with wife number two. Only that time he stood outside with Borger, both of them smoking his Luckies and watching half the antiques in Louisiana enter the front door of what was ski-chalet look-alike senior housing, transformed to faculty housing due to falling enrollment. Armoires and chests and rocking chairs, gilded mirrors and drop-leaf tables, so much of it, and so heavy he thought it would surely fall through the industrial-carpet-covered plywood floors of what was essentially cheap, early seventies construction work.

Now it was Luckies again, bought for the occasion, this time standing without Borger, inside to smoke them on the sturdy hardwood floors of the top apartment in an old, not-so-well-maintained college-owned house across the street from the campus entrance. And to be fair, she was moving half an apartmentful of stuff to an apartment half the size of the one she was moving from, and so of course it would look like a lot. At least he could put down a bottle of beer wherever he damn well pleased, and no one was going to panic and screech at him about rings and coasters. Not Ellie.

Her furniture was not so different from his. Used, as opposed to antique. An old, fat, pseudo-ugly dresser, a gouged and rickety Chinesey-looking bedside table. A new, however, bed, consisting of queen-size mattress and box spring that would double as a frame and would replace the saggy twin he'd named Old Squeaky. Also speakers, an amplifier, tape deck, and turntable, so he could listen once again to his seventy-eight collector jazz albums; and her TV was a definite improvement over the monster black-and-white a student had unloaded on him before a summer break. He had to allow for the fact that there were some definite advantages here, too.

To compensate for volume and plants. And here came another one, a feathery-looking drooping one she was carrying past him into the bedroom. Probably had plans to hang it from the ceiling so it could drop little dried-up droopy feathers all over whatever was beneath it. His desk, he'd betcha. Plants always came with women, even if the women weren't moving in. Like Hilary, he remembered, who brought to his other post and prenuptial apartment some green thing. Swore it was indestructible short of being plastic. It had lasted one week, maybe two — green, that was. Stayed there on the same bookcase, brown, for about a year, even after she was long gone, until one day he noticed it again and took the trouble to throw it out, cute little handmade pottery pot and all.

He put out his cigarette in one of his baseball-souvenir ashtrays. He lit another one. More boxes, labeled kitchen, labeled bedroom, labeled kitchen, kitchen, bedroom, miscellany, and books, books, books. All of them piled in one room only, the living room, middle of the three, the only one the movers could put something down in and not block their access to the door they kept going out of and coming back in through.

A father, the son, and the hired hand. Same family-run company who'd moved him off the curb after some costly negotiation since it was against company policy to move any possessions that were not actually under a roof. "What company?" he'd said. "What company? A father, a son, and a lackey or two? Give me a break, man, I'm out on the street." So they'd moved him into wife number one's basement and attic, then they'd moved him into this attic, which was what this apartment essentially was. And now, their faces increasingly amused with each box, chair, and couch pillow they brought up, they were moving in the crazy professor's new main squeeze, the cause, he figured they figured, of all their previous business.

The father was too busy pissing and moaning to pay much attention, but the son, sure to be taking over the business shortly, if not on this very day, considering how the father, paunchy and red-faced, was coughing and spitting, definitely looked entertained. And the young smooth-muscled Hispanic employee could barely contain himself, looked like he was near to pissing his pants with each box he'd dump on top of the box he'd dumped before it. Kept moving a toothpick from one corner of his mouth to the other, like that might keep him from laughing outright. Until he just couldn't restrain himself, and said, "Man? Where are you gonna put all this shit?"

And Babineau, close to saying, down your throat, along with your fucking toothpick, shrugged and said: "She'll figure it out. Women are good at that."

And Ellie, just up from another run to her car, holding yet another jungle in front of her face, said through it as she walked between them, "It'll be fine. It's not a lot, really. It just looks like it, but it's not," and moved on by to reveal an unimpeded view of her posterior self.

Then Babineau detected a distinct change in atmosphere. Suddenly — what was it? The guy wasn't acting so damn superior anymore. The son, too, who'd just joined them, box-in-arms, to make it a threesome. Babineau could swear it was empathy, mutual understanding, as they gazed, with near funereal sobriety, at the doorway through which she'd momentarily disappeared. Because they knew, had to admit, that this is what you did, this is what they all did, had to do, if they were going to get themselves laid on a regular basis.

Still, he wasn't going to lift a finger. Let them sweat it out. He could take their ridicule and condolences both, while the clutter and pelf rose to his knees, his ears, goddamnit, while he kissed good-bye those wide empty floors the dustballs had traversed like tumbleweed. They'd get their cold cash upon completion of contract, the father, the son, and the lackey. No question. But he'd get the girl.

And her cat. The only thing he'd really balked at.

"Please, Babineau," she'd said. "He's not so bad."

The roommate couldn't take him because the boyfriend she was moving in with had a Great Dane. And you'd think the Dane would want to eat the cat, but it was the other way around.

And that was one of many reasons why he loathed them. The beagle puppy he'd been given as a boy, rendered one-eyed by one of those useless pieces of protoplasm. He remembered how it had looked, and the sound the dog made. And the sound the cat made when later that summer it had come running to him in his back-yard, orange and black and white. Calico, he remembered, all soft-ness and affection, slipping through and around his legs like a fuck-ing coral snake.

He'd grabbed it. Done his best to strangle it, well out of his mother's earshot, and failed. That will too fierce for his small hands.

He had liked, it was true, one cat, belonging to his children when he'd last lived with them. A big tom who still had his balls attached. A prodigious hunter who'd kept a respectful distance. Maybe he could strike up some kind of similar rapport with this one, brown-black with yellow eyes, whom she'd named Masai, after the African tribe that only drank milk and blood. Spooky in itself, and what kind of creature had yellow eyes that wasn't sinister?

This one pissed in her beloved plants. And she forgave it. Broke a little glass something. Forgave it again. This thing: good for noth-ing but eating canned glop and scraping around in its stinky little sandbox when it wasn't spread the length of the windowsill to stare at him through slitted pupils, and with the smugness of an organism at the foot of the food chain who knew it had the power to maim the top guns. Felines.

But they coexisted, until one day the thing tripped him up once again, in the middle of a workout when he was carrying a plate in each hand to add to the others on his dumbbells for three sets of curls. So he grabbed it by the throat, raising it slowly, at arm's length, to eye level, and held it there for a moment, so it would know who was boss, and to marvel, too, at how, unlike the last time he'd tried this death grip, he could maintain it.

He let go, launched it to the sound of its and Ellie's screams combined. He'd been aiming through the bedroom doorway, but the cat had clipped the doorjamb with a good thunk and hadn't landed on its feet. And when it got to them, it disappeared. For good. Must have hid, until it seized the opportunity of an open door or screenless window to escape to a more hospitable environment.

Babineau had to hand it to the thing. Once it got the picture, it knew what it had to do to save its ass. Survival instinct.

Which was something like what he said to her — that it would be all right, it would survive — when after three days of flyers and newspaper notices, and diurnal and nocturnal hunts in neighbors' yards, she walked in and sat down on the unsteady-legged living room loveseat, put her hands over her face and was so still and quiet, he couldn't tell if she was angry, or sad, or even breathing.

He waited, standing between kitchen and living room, holding the spoon he'd been using to stir the baked beans he planned to eat with the frying keilbasa and eggs he'd cooked sunnyside in the grease, but she didn't respond.

Finally she said, "I really loved that cat." The tone, not angry, so he could breathe easy about that. Sad, yes, but the whole demeanor, the use of the past tense; it was surrender. She'd finally conceded to that ungrateful conglomeration of differentiated cells, about as loyal and affectionate as a protein-eating plant. And he wanted to tell her, did tell her then, that really, it had not wanted to be found. That "that's why things run away, Little Cabbage," he said. "They don't want to be where they were." Still, she just sat there, and so he decided to check his beans and turn his sausage, and told her he'd made enough so she wouldn't have to pick at his, and figured he could feel confident that things would at least get back to normal around there.

eleven

He will ask her to marry him, and she will accept, sitting on his weight bench by the bedroom doorway, just about to untie her running shoes.

"Makes sense," he says, "going to visit my family at Christmas. Might as well make it a honeymoon. It'll go over better with my mother anyway. Us being married and all." He talks to her from the living room, closing the windows against the first serious fall chill. Good for running, but cooling them off too fast, now that they've stopped. Finally, no more windows to push down, bang, he turns and faces her, hands on hips, chest hair glistening, a red bandanna tied Indian style around his head, white teeth in the center of his dark beard. He's wearing puffy, old, red-nylon shorts and the lining is poking out from the crotch. They'd doubled for a bathing suit in the summertime, small for his gut, but just right for the slender sturdy legs he stands on, spread slightly, like they might have been when he stood before his troops. Planted. Like nothing much could knock him over.

She looks at him, loving how he looks. Those bright teeth, and the bandanna, his sharp nose. That chest and stance. He positively shines sometimes, everything that is in him rising like something from dark water. Startling. The flash and flick and gone. Like his eyes in hers, too quick for the whole message, a positive ID.

"So what do you think, Little Cabbage?" he says. "You think you want to marry this demon-ridden, frog-bodied, pencil-peckered old fart?"

"I do," she says.

"And we'll make some babies together, you and I. Damn fine babies," he says.

"Yes," she says, beaming. "We'll make some babies." Just beaming. Even when she's alone there, still sitting on the bench, sweat drying, and sneakers still tied, listening to his pee hit the toilet water, and the fart that follows. Still, she's smiling. She can feel it there on her face, like a new and astounding physical feat, because it feels like it has exceeded the breadth and duration of all the other ones she's ever made.

She has never been so happy. Only babies to go now. That accomplished, her life will be completed, and then all she'll have to do is live it.

part two

twelve

Outside, and in the awful heat of Alabama, Ellie Rifkin bent down to pick up a caterpillar. It was green, neon green. Even the little, tiny palm-tree shaped bristlelike things that it was covered with were uniformly green, and they tilted, like two separate coconut groves, toward and away from each other with the caterpillar's immediate resumption of its journey — even if it was to be made now, not in the wiry, suburban, curbside grass, but across the smooth and potentially threatening expanse of an open human hand.

"Look. Look, Lithe," Ellie said, and glanced up to see if she'd heard, if both Lithe and Babineau had heard, saw they were still walking, so she called again, "Lithe, look," wanting to say, didn't she think it looked like one of those sticky little giggly creatures from a toy-store bin? Didn't it? she'd say, smiling. But then she felt a hotness in her hand, all around and inside the inside of her hand, that surpassed the sweaty and persistent hot she always felt in this place if she ventured out of any enclosed structure: cars, houses, stores that were eternally climate controlled, made habitable only by the existence of AC.

This was different. This heat felt as if her hand produced it, and was, in fact, rapidly turning up the thermostat, feeling now like it would leave a scorch mark on anything it touched. It could have been glowing and growing, expanding into a fat, red deformity of itself, but when she looked at it, she saw nothing that would indicate the small agony she was in. Her palm was pale, smooth, even cool looking, still wide open for maximum surface area, and still raised for the original purpose of examining the caterpillar who was now methodically approaching the little gully at the start of the middle finger.

"Ow," she said. "Ow," and gave a flick.

"Okay, Mommy?" Lithe said, her face just next to Ellie's, if not a little higher, since Ellie still squatted.

"I don't know," she said, wishing she could have controlled the reflex that had sent the caterpillar flying. It might not have been the caterpillar's fault, after all. She'd never heard of an aggressive caterpillar, only those that tasted bad to birds, and those that imitated the coloration of the bad-tasting caterpillars, so the birds would not eat them, too. Or maybe that was when they became butterflies. All in all though, it was still pretty tame.

"Okay, Mom?" Babineau said, taking up his daughter's concern. Ellie could see his white jeans, his well-polished cowboy boots.

"I don't know," she said again, and shook her hand like maybe that would make it okay, and hoped her racing heart and constricting throat were simply physiological signs of her distress at having been mysteriously poisoned, and not the precursor to the imminent and swift destruction of her nervous system. "It was just a caterpillar," she said. "It was neat. It was all green. Really bright. There," she said, spotting it without even trying to, and pointing to where it still traveled, same pace, same direction, apparently unfazed by its recent capture and catapult, if not a little smug, now back on its rightful terrain.

"A caterpillar?" Babineau said

"There," she said. "See, Lithe? I think it stung me. It stung me, I think," she said, back to examining her hand, and again seeing nothing to indicate what it felt like. Not even a small welt. Nothing. "I've never heard of a stinging caterpillar," she said, and looked up at Babineau, who was smiling. "Caterpillars don't sting," she said. And then he started laughing, and she might have joined in, seeing that since she wasn't dead, her predicament was a little comical, but his laugh wasn't particularly kind or inviting — amused, maybe, but not really affectionate. She'd heard it before. He made the sound to precede a point that he would momentarily iterate, which was sure to prove, beyond a doubt, that she was a fool. He always milked the moment, forcing his forced laugh to continue long after anyone else would consider it appropriate to stop. Gloating. Poor sportsmanship, if you asked her.

She waited, on her knees now, head bowed to look at her hand, of course, but ironically conforming her body into the perfect pose for the felling of the axe. "What is it, Babineau?" she said, resigned, unprotesting, wanting to exemplify, as always, those who had the grace to laugh at themselves. But still, she was unable to hide from her voice, all the irritation she felt.

He laughed a little more, and then said finally, "And you thought nature was so fucking benevolent. Ha!" he said. "My little pantheistic wood nymph. My northern-born, East Coast, liberalized, Green Peace, nature girl," and still laughing started back across the street, eager, she was sure, to tell those he'd join there of her foolish exploit, but walking unhurried, walking just as he had before she'd called him back. Continuing on his way, much like the caterpillar — who'd known from the beginning of its secret advantage, who'd known, of course, from the beginning that she'd posed no threat to it at all.

She was starting to hate it there. And wanted to shout that at him, that she hated it there. Stinging caterpillars, for God's sake. Fire ants. And the heat.

The heat. The first time she felt it was at the precise moment she'd stepped from the train's refrigerated interior onto the bright, empty concrete platform of the small, deserted, and rather unremarkable red-brick station, given that they'd traveled one day, one night, and most of the next day to get there. Get to what felt like a place on another planet. One with an orbit closer to the sun, and that could not possibly support human life, so that the woman who approached her, walking quickly, breathing naturally, healthy, smiling even, could not really be human, just looked it, a humanoid-type organism with a whole different thermal chemistry.

"Hot," was all Ellie could say to her. "It's very hot here," she said squinting, holding Lithe on her hip, feeling Lithe's arm already sticking to her own. That was really all she could think to say to this woman's welcome. Margaret? Is that what she'd said? She'd thought it was Marilyn, if she was who she thought she was. Very tall. Very slender, wearing lipstick, and black-lensed large-framed sunglasses, blue cotton trousers, blue canvas flats, a crispy white sleeveless blouse, and when she waved to Babineau who stood by the train getting their luggage, Ellie noticed the armholes were big enough to reveal the top edge of the side of her white bra.

Ellie wasn't wearing one. She'd stopped soon after she'd started, not on any political grounds, a logical assumption, since it had been the early seventies, but because they were a nuisance: straps slipping, elastic itching and gripping hard enough to interfere with her digestion. So, small-breasted anyway, she wore undershirts, or nothing. Like today, nothing but the sentimental, well-faded, half-shrunk, scoopneck little turquoise T-shirt she'd had for six years at least, and had chosen to wear yet again that morning somewhere in Virginia, and wished now, very much, that she hadn't, that she'd changed, bothered to better brush and clip back her hair, maybe put on a little makeup. Because all she could think about was how short she was, how young looking, how hot it was, and how her pokey nipples were poking straight at this woman's midriff, this woman who was so tall and friendly, and, Ellie was fairly certain, head of the Philosophy department, the one who'd invited Babineau to be the guest chair for, she'd written, three short months at a big university in a small southern town.

Ellie was so hot. And it was so bright there, after all those hours behind tinted windows. She wanted some sunglasses as wide and dark as the woman's, but could only shift Lithe a little more to the front of her, temporarily, she knew, because Lithe was becoming deadweight heavy, and soon she'd put her down fast, when her arms reached the limit of their capacity and tripped to automatic release, protests or not, and even if Lithe was barefooted. Maybe a little pavement sizzle would get her to get those shoes on fast next time because she sure couldn't, defeated as she'd been by the kicks and screams and contortions, and looks from other passengers, and the swift-approaching station stop.

God, she felt stupid standing there, holding her barefoot daughter, braless, short, thick thighed and stunned by heat and by the fact that she was really there, that she had actually arrived there, in a place where the air she breathed was hotter than the lining of her lungs, her eyes squinting near to shut as her only means of protection from a sun that would, if it did not blind her first, kill her eventually.

"So you're Babineau's wife." the woman said. "I've heard so much about you," and raising her voice to baby tones, she said, "And you must be little Lithe."

"Say, hi, Sweety," Ellie said, relieved the woman's attention had shifted, though she was curious as to what, exactly, Babineau had said about her. Because he said such nice things about her to people like this woman. She would have liked to have known exactly what they were. "She's a little shy," Ellie said to excuse her daughter having abruptly turned her face away from the woman to press it hard into Ellie's shoulder. "Not all the time," she said. "Just now, I guess," and thanked God that Babineau was finally approaching them — bags on the cart — because he would be sure to do all the talking now, after he was finished giving the woman the big bear hug he was giving her. Marilyn. It was Marilyn.

Because he said, "Marilyn! Finally! My advocate, my sponsor. My ticket to the South and liberator from financial bondage. We finally meet."

The woman laughed, but Ellie cringed. He should, she thought, at least pretend he'd come there for more than the money. But Babineau could always get away with it, his obvious disdain for social conventions, and his blunt reversals of them, perceived even by the most conservative as charming; forgiven and dismissed as one of the many eccentricities that go hand in hand with brilliance.

She relaxed. He was talking. They were laughing, the story to explain Lithe's bare feet, made funny, though he'd told her at the time to hurry up, to stop being so rough, and she'd said, "You try then. You try."

But she would never give her version. His was better, even had her smiling a little, too, as she followed them to the car. But then her arms gave out. And Lithe was standing on the pavement in front of her, arms round Ellie's thighs, demanding that Ellie pick her up, pick her up, saying her feets, her feets hurt, while Babineau pulled farther ahead, talking, talking, pushing the luggage cart, lifting a hand now and then from the bar to emphasize a point, until he finally heard her calling to him to please take Lithe. "Take her, please," she said, suddenly caught and embarrassed by the tearfulness, the shaky panic in her voice. Because she really — now that she was there — knew she didn't want to be. She didn't want to be at all. And when the train began to move, so sleek, and shiny, and cool looking, the great sound of the engine fading to reveal the gentle, slow, and slowly accelerating click-click of its departure, she watched it go with the sad and injured gaze of the abandoned and deceived.

Only once they'd reached the house did she cheer up a little, the effect of spotting yet another insect, her very first encounter with southern fauna, this one a grasshopper-locust-type thing, as big as a small mammal, mottled orange and black, and sitting in the center of a flagstone, in the center of the flagstone walk, like it was there to deliver a message. But it was Babineau who spoke, saying, "Holy shit. That thing could feed a small tribe of Bushmen." Just like him to consider it something to ingest, like doves, squirrels, like the pheasants who would wander up or dart across the long driveway of the newly built house they'd just left. "Dinner," he'd say.

"Garden Devil," the woman, Marilyn, said from behind her.

"God-awful nuisances, those things," she said, reminding Ellie of how, with a little familiarity, the exotic can so quickly change.

"It's very big," Ellie said.

"That's how they make 'em down here, Little Cabbage. Big. Big bugs," said Babineau.

"Big bug," said Lithe, who'd been standing beside Ellie, watching it all along. Then, "There go," she said when, without any display of its intention to do so, it leaped, landing with a sound near to a thump, and with greater force than its legs could absorb, stumbling — if insects can stumble — in grass that had been mowed, but not recently, that was covered with seedpods, and sticks, and blade-shaped leaves, all in different stages of decay, as if trees here did not shed seasonally, but continually, indefinitely.

There were two of them in the front of the house. Tall and weedy looking, they provided shade, a blessing, a necessity, Ellie guessed, but dropped their droppings on the path, too, the porch steps, porch roof and the main roof — which was likely the cause of Ellie's first impression of the house, when, from the backseat of Marilyn's car, and driving up the unexpected dirt road, off of what had been a typically suburban asphalt one, and on into the wooded cul-de-sac, she saw it. Neglected. That's how it looked. Big and white and solid looking with every reason to be loved, but not.

The inside was sadder, precisely because it was even nicer, big high-ceilinged foyer, large living room to the left, dining room straight ahead, the wall and banister of a staircase slanting upward on her right to a wide window at the landing; clean, beige wall-to-wall carpeting, newly painted white walls, clean white gauze curtains. But the dining room table was direct from a university cafeteria: round, flesh-colored, chipped Formica, cigarette scarred, gum certain to be stuck beneath; the shiny, tan, half-moon backs of four metal folding chairs rising above the flat circumference. In the living room a wood-framed Queen Anne yellow velveteen couch, like something that had been in an administrator's waiting room, or an alumni lounge, and once worn and dated, had been moved off of someone's mind by being moved here, and paired with a nappy pale-green wing chair, joined by an orange, canvas butterfly chair, a bench coffee table in the center of them all, chunks of laminated wood missing from the legs, and the rest of the room empty, except for a television.

And standing in the doorways, walking through bedrooms, or really, rooms with beds in them, a big old-fashioned white-and-black tiled bathroom, and back down the stairs, Ellie wanted to like it, Ellie tried to like it, it being so big and clean and sturdy. But she couldn't, conceding without much of a struggle that any attempt to accomplish what she'd figured would be the first thing to occupy her here, would be met with failure. She could not possibly — given her resources, the big empty blank walls, naked shelves and mantle piece, the big empty blank floors, and the temporary nature of her and Babineau and Lithe's occupancy — make this house a home. This house, so worthy of care and appreciation, going to waste even as she lived in it.

First thing she did, though, was stick up some of Lithe's marker scribble drawings, after she'd finally remembered to buy some tape. But she'd had to laugh at how silly they looked there. Little tiny drawings stuck on a wall with dimensions suited to a gilt-framed portrait of some austere southern ancestor. Pathetic, she thought, but she didn't take them down. They were Lithe's after all, the drawings still representing some claim to the place, even if it was as tenuous as the tape's adhesive.

Second thing she did was go outside and inspect the backyard bushes, any flowering shrubs that might be of interest, something she could, perhaps, nurture to health, but this small forage was cut short by a terrible sensation of burning, all up and down her bare legs. Her second encounter with southern fauna: the ants, so aptly named for fire, who, she discovered, too late, were the inhabitants of the curious football shaped eruption of clay-colored earth in the center of the small square of fenced lawn. "Jesus fucking Christ," she screamed, running and slapping and yanking Lithe along with her, back into the dim, and eternally cool, stale, recirculated air of the big and empty house, where, it seemed, she would just have to stay.

Three weeks later, you'd think she might have thought twice then, before picking up that caterpillar. And so thought Ellie, getting slowly to her feet, disgusted with herself. And finally beaten. Babineau was right. He was always right. She had thought nature was benevolent, had thought so for years and had turned to it always, from childhood on, for solace. All because of a geographic proximity to a gentler more beatific ecosystem. That was all. Nothing deeper, more spiritual about it. And walking across the street, she vowed to keep her hands to herself, damned if she'd touch another living thing down there and trigger a newer and nastier mechanism of defense than those that had already harmed her.

thirteen

She is praying again, and it reminds her of Lithe, and of herself, when she was little, asking for something from her mother, something she'd seen in a department store, and had to have, just had to have, certain that if she was for once, just this once victorious, she would never, ever want anything, ever again.

Same now — if he lived. If he just lived, she really couldn't imagine wanting anything more. And who could she request this from but God? Because saving Babineau at this juncture was beyond her practical application. Still, though, she felt stupid saying the word: *God*. Like an impostor, since He was not her territory, never had been. Stupid, too, that her conception of the thing she was addressing was some big man up there in the sky, who she could entreat to do her will. How unimaginative.

It was a woman who told her, a woman doctor who Ellie had never seen before, and would never see again, like she'd become manifest for this message alone, like an angel, or a prophet, or a trickster. Ellie couldn't know which at the time, only that she had the kind of hair Ellie would have chosen if she didn't have her own. It was blue-black, short, and glossy, moving with the slightest motion of her head. And she had small, thin, hands, reddish and veiny, folded one on the other, like she might be trying to generate some heat because they looked cold, like they'd be cold and wet feeling in Ellie's hand when the doctor stood and shook, as

Ellie expected her to, once she was finished saying whatever it was she was saying — in a way that made Ellie feel like she'd said the same thing to a lot of people, but had never heard it said to her, had never tried to imagine it being said to her, speaking as she was with her knees pressed tight, and from the other end of the hard, hallway bench, like she meant to put some distance between them.

Not till then did Ellie know there was a chance of it. Not after he'd been cleaned and wrapped, pinned and screwed and hung in place, so that all he had to do was fuse and harden. Time. It would just take time. That was all she thought they were up against. Not this. This had come as a surprise. And she said, "I didn't know you could die from broken bones." To which the doctor said, "Well, he's got a lot of them," and something about how what was in them was out of them and in places it shouldn't be, gumming up the works.

So what could she do but pray? Sitting beside him watching his chest go up, go down, and being thankful each time. But the more she sat there among bodies and machines, the more undifferentiated they became, each requiring near equal attention from the nurses for any number of things that needed fiddling and adjustment. One simply took over for the other where the other fell short, did not perform up to par or at full capacity. And the more she sat there, the more ludicrous her prayerlike pleas became. Because what it came down to was flesh and bone. Either it eventually functioned or it didn't. Either he was beyond repair, or he wasn't. Totaled or salvageable. And nothing she could beg for into the air that she was calling God would have much to do with it.

fourteen

"William Loman," he said. "That's who I am. I'm Willie the fuck Loman," he said, feeling inspired. Perfect, he thought, sitting in his boxers, on his desk chair, in the one room his most present wife had allowed him. She called it his study, but he knew better. Quarantined again. What was it exactly? So offensive was he, that he had to be confined, like some kind of house pet, best kept behind baby gates with spread newsprint for the pissing? Well, fuck that. Fuck that. "Willie Loman," he bellowed and hoped she was listening. Listening and quaking there in that bed she was pretending to sleep in on the other side of the bright-lit bathroom that, doors ajar, connected one room to the other.

He bent over and plunged his left arm, elbow deep into his left boot. Scooped barehanded a heaping portion of polish, slapped it to the leather, and scrubbed: back, front, sides, top, toe, like he was meaning to take something off rather than put something on. "Naught for all and all for naught," he said, then paused, the need for his cigarette, lit and balanced in the ashtray, the rapidly warming beer beside it, suddenly pressing. But one hand deep within calfskin, the other stained the sticky tar brown he'd seen on the fingertips of smokers far more committed to the pleasure than he, he found himself momentarily stymied, halted by a dilemma that suddenly took precedence over the one that had inspired his proud literary allusion. Until he finally thought to extract his arm from boot, to find there a hand at the end of it, sufficiently clean and useable to assist him in the resumption of what had been this evening's primary occupation, begun hours ago in the company of students, at a patio table, under a tropical sky, with the potent contribution of tequila, in shot form, cut by salt and lime. Now its effects, prolonged by many a bottle of beer, seemed to be winding down, further quashed by the subtle, yet palpable presence of feminine disapproval. Sure poison, he knew, to even the most blissful of buzzes, which this one had not been. Not even at its outset.

He took a drag-to-last, filled his cheeks with beer, swallowed twice to get it down, raised his boot and turned it this way and that, until he was certain he'd not missed a spot, belched a good one, then took up a well-used chamois, thinking that if he were to blow out his brains, he'd do it spit-shined, by God. And spit. And shined. Spit and shined, spit and shined, and remembered — her.

"Hear me, Little Cabbage?" Man, it was a long time he'd been calling her that, butchering the French by making it into English, just to show her she was taking three-month leave of him in her third college year, to live in a place where people called their loved ones cabbages. And it had stuck — for so long now, he hardly knew he said it anymore, until some newcomer asked its origin.

"Little Cabbage," he said. Silence. "You do know who Willie Loman is, do you not?" He waited, chamois poised. Then there. That didn't take so long. When it came to that little ego of hers, she took the bait like a regular piranha. Muffled, weary, but definitely audible, she answered in the affirmative: "Yes, Babineau. I know who Willie Loman is."

"Well, then," he resumed his work on the boot. "Seeing as how you know who Willie Loman is, then you must know as well, of Willie Loman's sad end. And seeing as how I am on this night, as the headshrinkers say, identifying with him, why is it that you remain incommunicado, feigning sleep over there, a room apart from me, so that I find myself speaking not to a warm sympathetic wife, but to a bathroom light?"

"I am not feigning sleep."

"Ah, but you are avoiding the question."

"So what would you have me do, Babineau?"

"Pretty sad now I should have to be the one to tell you. Pretty fucking sad. I'm in pain here, and you're asking me what you should do?"

"As far as I can *smell*, Babineau, you've been doing a pretty good job of dulling it."

"And you can smell far, L. C. I'm impressed; and at the very clever way you've called me a drunk, so absolving yourself of all responsibility for any self-destructive act I may just decide to commit tonight. However, this imbibement, this drunkenness, you so coldly accuse me of, does not diminish the fact that I am in pain here. That I find myself an aging pseudo-satirist fast sliding downward on what others may perceive to be a mountain of a career, but what I see as something that has left me with not a pot to piss in. A failure as a provider, failure as a husband and father. Willie Loman material.

"You are not a failure, Babineau," she said, sounding like she was reading aloud in poor light.

"Thank you, my good wife. I feel all better now." He spit on the back of the boot heel and rubbed. "Now you go on and get your beauty rest. Even the remotest flicker of compassion, to one such as yourself, I know, can be highly taxing."

"Babineau — "

"No, no. Really. You go ahead. Sleep. Your kind of sympathy I do not need." And be damned — she did. Just a pitiable last *Oh, Babineau* out of her, then silence and so he had to assume she'd gone ahead and made the big Zs. He couldn't believe it. Well, no, he could. Fuck'er, he thought, and raised and scrutinized his boot to pronounce this part of the process done. Good. Now for the part that was his favorite.

He picked up the buffing brush that still, he marveled, had more bristles in it than he had hair, though it was old enough to have belonged to his father, along with the whole shoeshine kit it came from, made of some hardwood, like oak, divided into compartments designed just to fit what they were meant to hold. As durable and useful and aesthetically pleasing as all the other things relegated for display, if he so chose, in this one room only: boots, hats, pipes, lighters, knives, and guns. Things made to last, requiring cleaning, oiling, sharpening, shaping. Things made of steel, wood, and leather, and by nothing but the human hand.

No way would he go anywhere without them. Even taking on the laws of two states and negotiating bureaucratic hoops so he could now have at hand, snug in their cut-out foam cavities, and tight shut in their steel encased lockbox, his antique .32, snubnosed .38, his Colt .22 single-action, his tiny .22 revolver, sized to fit whole in his open palm, as perfectly formed in miniature as a three-month-old fetus, and the king of all calibers, the .45 automatic, fucking cannon of a firearm. Definitely the one to employ were he to make good on his literary parallel, in no way wanting to risk survival with a brain reconfigured into the shape of a doughnut.

He'd had to have his guns. Damn near un-American to be without one, particularly in the South. The South, too, being where he'd learned to handle them, the one thing his father taught him hands-on, with a patience and decency, Babineau had suspected even then, was more for the benefit of the gun he'd used, than him. But no matter. If Babineau was anything at this point, he was a hell of a shot.

And he hadn't really minded Yes Siring and No Siring, Officer Sir, the state troopers he'd spoken to. State police were a good military outfit, mostly made up of ex-Marines, trained to respond with the same kind of precision and quick action as the weapons they carried. A clean life, the military. No gray areas. The only five full years of his, when he'd woken up, knowing exactly what he was supposed to do that day. And he'd been wondering how it would feel again, even wishing at times, wishing now, as he sat buffing his boot to a shine that would exceed the standards of any military inspection, that he'd never left. Would likely have remained a captain, maybe still be married to wife number one, certainly he'd be retired, good pension as opposed to the pissant pittance of academia, all the time in the world to do the brain work he hadn't had enough time for then. He'd have seen active duty — no matter he'd opposed that war — a few shrapnel wounds and a Purple Heart for proof. Who knows? Maybe he'd have been a fucking hero. Or dead. All he knew was that lately, whenever he saw those dress blues on any dumb-ass soldier in any second-rate mall, he saw something he wanted.

fifteen

Where do things go when they are lost?

"Where could it be?" she said to Babineau, who answered her by telling her to pray to Saint Anthony.

"That's your department," she said, sounding more scornful than she'd expected. But he could do better than that, couldn't he? Hold her? Hug her? At least look at her instead of at his feet that he was, at the moment, shedding of bright red socks, sitting in his underwear at the edge of their bed. He could tell her she'd find it, it'd turn up, not to worry. Or that he'd buy her another just as nice. But what was she thinking? He hadn't even bought her her wedding ring; nothing made from precious metal or stone and the sweat, as he said, of the exploited.

Maybe it was just that he didn't wear one himself. Not surprising Babineau's body voltage would be a notch higher than everyone else's. At least this was her theory as to why every watch he wore went haywire. So he used a pocket watch. Nothing fancy, coincidentally suited to his cowboy getup and love of ritual, the pulling of it out, clicking of it open, clicking of it shut, executed with such measure and grace, and unhurried flourish, he fairly stopped time itself.

Ellie, on the other hand, being more like most, could wear one on her wrist. And in the few seconds it took her to glance, and register what it told her, she felt pleasure, always, at its beauty, so sleek, so shiny, and elegant, made by one of the finest Swiss companies, but least known in the States, a jeweler had told her. A real treasure, he'd said. And she'd considered it such, a gift from her mother, who'd bought it for her the year before, in Geneva.

Now it was gone. Its absence discovered with that jolt of horror born of sensation: the tiny wrist hairs stirred by blowing air, her sleeve touching skin never touched by her sleeve. Then the wish to be wrong in the time it took her right hand to arc through space and eyes to look downward to the spot, and confirm, hand now clasping wrist with a grip that could staunch blood, what she'd suspected. She said, "My watch. My watch is gone. Where's my watch?" Would have said it aloud even if Babineau had not been there to hear, the realization just too awful, too big to be contained inside her head alone.

But since Babineau was there, she now hoped he'd prove her wrong, tell her he'd seen it on the bathroom sink, the back of the toilet, her bedside table. But he only said, "You sure?"

"Yes, yes, I'm sure," she said, crazily frisking herself and raising her bottom as best she could in a seatbelt, to feel the seat beneath. Another jump of her heart, and her hand jerked to her ears to nonsensically assure herself that her earrings had not met the same fate. Then she asked for the interior light, and next, her seatbelt was off and she was crouched to the floor, cheek pressed to the underside of the glove compartment, aware that in the event of a crash, her death would not be unlike one she'd meet in a metal compactor, but determined anyway to attain the longest reach over and all around the gummy carpet of the well-used three-month lease they'd contracted that very day.

And this, their very first night, spent out at a recommended restaurant, eating shrimp and gumbo and catfish, drinking wine and laughing proudly at Lithe who demanded, got, and ate her whole plate of fried frog legs. Such fun. Good restaurant, Babineau jolly and expansive, virtual buddies with their young and handsome waiter by the end of the meal — eaten with a view of the river named, of course, for an exterminated Indian chief, and said to be so polluted it would blister the skin of anyone fool enough to touch the black, slow-moving water that Ellie thought beautiful, the few trees at its banks that were not immolated by kudzu, bending toward it like they believed it offered sustenance.

So where could it have gone? The strap had not been frayed. The pins, as far as she knew, snug in place. Still, it had to have fallen somewhere. Under the restaurant table, maybe. So she'd have to go back. That night. But Babineau had already taken one wrong turn in this new town, on these unfamiliar roads, in the dark, and she, not having done the driving, hadn't paid attention, and the restaurant somewhere on the outskirts and over a bridge, she'd never find it, and if she did, it might by then be closed.

"Call," Babineau said.

The question, the long wait in the harsh-lit, narrow-laned kitchen, phone to ear through which she heard the clink of glassware, voices, laughter, all the same sounds of festivity she'd heard when she'd been there to add to them. Now they were offensive to her, like they should have stopped out of a sense of courtesy.

"No Ma'am," she heard then. "He didn't find anything resembling a watch."

"Did he look under the table?"

"I'm sure he did, Ma'am."

"Well, please, could you just ask him?"

"I'll ask," the manager said, sounding now a little put upon. And more wait while she had to trust that he did, and the waiter maybe looked, and Babineau called to her from upstairs to tell her Lithe wanted her and not him to put her to bed. And just as she was yelling the last of: she'd be there in a minute, she heard again, No, the waiter had not found it, but he'd be happy to take her name and number, the manager's polite detachment, his runny accent, and Babineau, having not heard her, calling for her again, enough to make her infuriated, along with the fact that she did not know what her phone number was, had been told that the one typed in the middle of the dial was wrong, and earlier, had not even been able to call the restaurant without having to ask an operator for instructions; all of this reminding her that she was a stranger in a strange land, which made the prospect of finding something she'd lost in it that much more hopeless.

"How will I tell my mother?" she said, getting into bed while she glanced at the bedside table, again, because she couldn't not look.

"Don't," Babineau said. He was already in bed, cover pulled smooth, pinned to the mattress by his elbows, bent to hold up a fat and heavy book wrapped in a serious-looking navy-blue dust jacket. He wouldn't be going to sleep for hours, though, this, just one activity of the many that would follow it until his sleeping pill took effect, if it took effect, around two A.M.

She'd seen him swallow it, known he'd figured that her upset had done in any possibility for some post-dinner-out sex, and she hadn't stopped him. Relieved, maybe. A little sad. Because she wanted something. Something. That she'd asked for before often enough, described, demonstrated, and what Babineau had come up with after the last long and arduous battle, felt like the pat he might give their dog when he told him he was a good dog. "Not in my reper-fucking-toire, I guess," he'd said to her, then, "Man, I can make you so hot, you scream for mercy and now you're sitting there, all pinchfaced and dissatisfied. I mean, what the fuck!" And as she remembered, had walked out before she could answer.

But she'd had no answer and even if now she miraculously thought of one, she would keep it to herself, because she felt his restlessness, the temporariness of his presence there beside her, the self-importance of his big, fat book. A dinner out was enough to make her whole evening, but he had lots of evening to go, and she wished to say that to him: to just go.

She leaned back on the pillows and picked up her own book, still wondering: Should she tell her mother now? Wait until she saw her again, knowing she would not, as Babineau had suggested, lie by omission, especially if she was certain to get caught. Because, sure enough, not seeing it, her mother would ask where the watch was. And really, Ellie knew she could tell her without too painful a consequence. There'd be that disappointed look, which would be the worst of it, and then she'd say something like, well, those things happen, and that would be all — except for the one thing, the one thing Ellie realized was what she was afraid of: that her mother would think she hadn't cared enough about the watch to have taken good care of it.

And how would she convince her mother otherwise? How could she possibly prove she loved a thing that wasn't there?

And so it was, that the next morning, Ellie did find her way to the restaurant, knowing it would not have yet opened, intending only to look in the parking lot, which was deserted, so still and quiet and bright, it was like a place different from the place she'd been the night before, private, and a little spooky, making her half-expect someone to appear suddenly and admonish her for trespassing.

But she stayed. She kept Lithe strapped into her car seat with a lollipop for distraction, so she could look undistracted at her sandaled foot sweeping like a metal detector over and over the glaring white gravel. Detecting nothing. And she was forced to conclude that yes, lost things have to go somewhere, but this thing was not where she would ever go again.

sixteen

The priest is the thing, she thinks, that she must get, if Babineau is doing what they say he is. That's what he'd want, isn't it? "A Father Delaney," he'd say, "a Father O'Leary. I don't give a shit. Just get me any ol' Irish teetotaler they're likely to provide on the premises, so I don't end up the Highway Haunter, L. C., stuck on some median strip to fuck up innocent motorists for all eternity."

And sure enough, he's got the red face, the white hair, but no girth and no height. He is a tiny and very, very old man. She has found him next to Gifts and Flowers, with relative ease, considering any other place she has tried to find in this great big hospital has taken her many more tries than one; directed to wings named for colors that they're not painted, riding on elevators whose doors close before her, and open behind her, so she feels she's been transported not three floors up, but to some giant conveyance, like a spaceship, or a satellite laboratory.

But the priest is just where they say he'll be, standing now, behind his desk, tilting his chin upward to study a computer print-out, taped to the top drawer of a four-tiered filing cabinet. He makes her feel enormous, like if she made one move, she'd knock something over, knock him over, trash the place. So she stands consciously still, her hands clasped below her new little belly, pulling her jumper taut around it, while she wonders why, at the mention of Babineau's name, the priest stopped her midsentence by standing up to turn and look at this sheet.

"Not there," he says.

"I'm sorry?"

"Babineau, Gerard, you say?"

"Yes. I mean, Gerard is his first name."

"Not on Gray 3."

"What do you mean?" she says. She unclasps her hands.

"This says he's not on Gray 3."

"But I was just there. With him. I came from there to here."

"Spell that again?" he says.

She is confused. This is not the kind of conversation she expected to have when she came here.

"Miss?" he says.

"Sorry. B-A-B-I-N-E-A-U."

He looks back to the sheet, holding the frames of his glasses as if to steady them like binoculars, and says, "Not there. He must be somewhere else."

"I really don't know what you're talking about," she says. "I mean, what are you talking about? Where does your list say he is?"

The priest looks at it again, looks down it, and up it. "It doesn't," he says.

"Well, then I guess your list needs updating because my husband has been here for three days. He has been on Gray 3 for three days, and I've been with him there for just about all that time, including only a few minutes ago, so I know where he is. I think I should know where he is."

The priest looks a little uncertain. "I don't believe it's outdated," he says.

"Who cares? Who cares?" she says. "Look," she says, "I've just been told my husband may be dying. Dying. And so I thought you should go there, you know, because he's Catholic, and give him the . . . you know, the . . . ," and she can't think of the name for it, realizes, face flushing hot, that the only reason she knows about it at all is from the movies. *On the Waterfront*. Karl Malden. He does it to someone in that movie, doesn't he? And she wonders if she's wrong, if she mixed it up with something else, or maybe the ritual isn't practiced anymore, like the Latin mass Babineau is always saying they should reinstate. But still, she can picture a priest standing at the foot of a bed, sprinkling water onto the bare feet of a near corpse, then closing the eyes when it is one, with a prayer and genuflection. She's just sure of it. The thing that gets you past Jail and directly to Boardwalk as Babineau might say. "*You* know," she says again to the priest, who's standing there looking like she's speaking in a language he thought he'd learned, but apparently, not well enough.

"God. I can't believe this," she says, clutching her head with her hands. And as if this has squeezed it from somewhere, she suddenly knows what she's been trying to remember, and yells it like a contestant at the buzzer. "Last rites," she says. "Give it to him."

But the priest only looks at her, his eyes all wide and rolly behind his fat, convex lenses and says, "Well, I'm sorry, Miss, but we'll have to find him first.

Babineau loved priests. He liked to call them Padre. Especially the ones a good ten to twenty years younger than he, just to make sure they knew how deep went his respect. All that sacrifice, all that deprivation.

There'd been one, especially, who he'd liked, who he met briefly under social circumstances at his mother's house on the fateful visit that had resulted in his messy union with wife number two. Father Peter, or something. Was a black belt in karate, young and handsome, strong and agile, with a delicacy about him, too, as Babineau remembered. Drove the parish women crazy. Even his mother, all atwitter: Can I get you this, Father; Can I get you that, Father. Didn't matter the age, all that languishing manhood, make any woman stick to her pants.

So he'd asked him, "Padre, how do you do it?" thinking it must hurt, literally, and the padre kind of smiled, revealing a dimple to kill, and said, "Well, that's how come I'm a black belt. That's how come I run ten miles a day. Anyone who would do that solely for recreation would be out of their mind."

Human, after all, Babineau thought, who, as a boy had considered the calling. Administering the host to his kneeling flock, reprimanding the altar boys, swinging the incense like a swagger stick. His life all laid out like a railroad track, no matter if they suddenly sent him to the Amazon, always funerals, always weddings, always Ash Wednesdays, Palm and Easter Sundays and Christmas Eves. Always, of course, customers at the confessional. These were the things you could count on. Nice digs, some sweet old lady to feed you. And no others — except those safely betrothed to Jesus — to make you feel like a pussy when you were the kind with more brain than bulk. Big vocabulary as opposed to biceps, and political as opposed to sexual savvy. Girls never knew what he was talking about. Just seemed — the few who listened — they liked how the talk sounded. Smart, shrewd, cynical, definitely more urbane than T-Beau Bilodeau, king of the football team, who he'd have rather been any day.

And so for a while he'd pondered it. Maybe he'd even become a Jesuit.

Studious, somber, clicking down quiet arched hallways, devoted to something that could only be good. How proud would be his mother. How disgusted and amused was his father, an Episcopalian, if he was anything, laughing that deep, wet, tobacco-made laugh, shaking his head and snapping his newspaper straight, and Babineau, just about out of the room when he said, "Sure to make your mother happy."

But of course his pecker prevailed. Not much of a battle when it's between pulling your pud while imagining its future adventures — or not. So he'd settled for the receiving end of things. He would open his mouth for the wafer, bow his head to catch the rim of the cup, join the United States Marine Corps. And this time, it was his mother stirring, stirring, her browning roux, who said, "Sure to make your father happy."

seventeen

*T*he gun was in his pocket. The little tiny .22, easily mistaken for a keychain ornament. Couldn't say it had the finest accuracy, but it was still the real thing, which the guy he pointed it at, later that night, would not believe.

"What the fuck's that? What the fuck's that?" he kept saying, this drunken asshole cracker, who'd been giving some black guy, come in for a quiet after-work beer, a hard time; followed him out of the bar when the guy tried to leave peaceably and then pushed him from behind and called him the N-word, which was when Babineau decided it was time to step in.

Bound to happen. Ellie gushing on about how much more integrated things were down there, how she could be the only white woman in a supermarket line, and the supermarket not necessarily in a designated ghetto space. How the South felt more like their territory, the whites more like visitors to it.

"Bullshit, honey," he'd said. And now this. Even in a college-town bar. He'd just been waiting for it to raise its ugly head.

"It's a gun, you stupid-assed motherfucker," he said. "What the fuck you think it is?"

"I dunno. Thought maybe it was your dick," he said and laughed. So pastey-faced pale, Babineau would have placed bets he'd be puking up his guts within the hour. He wore some too-short burgundy polyester pants, grabbed at the hips, gapped at the crotch, and one of those short-sleeved shirts, made to show the undershirt right through, accentuate the skinniness of the arms dangling like stretched putty out the blousy sleeves. What was this guy doing pushing people around?

"Man you got some big ones," Babineau said, duly impressed, figuring if he ever had a gun pointed at him, he'd be shitting bricks, which he was just about doing anyway, standing as he was at the other end of it. He said, "Now why don't you be a good ol' boy and just get along home. Sleep it off and leave this nice gentleman alone," not quite sure, as he spoke, where the nice gentleman was at the moment. Had to assume somewhere behind him, out of his peripheral vision, and not, he hoped, disappeared, leaving him with no excuse at all for doing what he was.

"Whatever you say, boss," the guy said, backing away, stumbling, smiling a little, nearly unconscious already, and so damn harmless Babineau wished the former cockiness back again, along with a knife, the one he was sure was coming after the push and the epithet, but which hadn't, as yet, put in an appearance.

"Now you ain't gonna shoot me now, are you, with that itty bitty thang, were I to just now slowly turn 'round so's I can walk without falling on my ass?"

"Hell no, buddy. I don't want to hurt no one. I just don't want no one to get hurt, get it?" Babineau said, sliding into Southern-speak, his mother tongue as easy as he could adopt any other. A whore of elocution was how he referred to himself, could talk to anyone the way they talked to him, a great diplomatic gift, even if it was unintentional, that had worked right now, the guy weaving a harmless retreat, leaving Babineau to stand there, feeling all eyes upon him, while he uncocked the hammer, as cooly as he could, all the while fearing his shaky hands might set the thing off, or worse, drop it with a clatter.

Safe in his pocket, he turned to the man he'd defended, not even sure, at this point, if he'd be able to pick him out, but then knew, right away, yes, it was him, the guy turning, too, away, in order to make a fast exit, as they say, before the curtain call. But aware he'd been caught, turning back, eyes down, eyes up, eyes down, a quick thank you, man, and then he was outta there. No handshake, pat-on-the-back, buy-you-a-beer kind of gratitude. More like he thought he was the next hit, Babineau being, as he was, armed and dangerous.

"Grateful motherfucker," Babineau said, and only then he saw the condition of his audience, his students, his new buddy and colleague Carl Rice, and various and assorted strangers, all looking at him, glassy-eyed, frozen, like they'd been struck by the worst Parkinsonian palsy.

He raised his hands. "Hey, just call me Charles the Fuck Bronson," he said. "The Vigilante Chair of our distinguished department." And slowly, with a good bit of persistence and a lot of elbow grease, he loosened them up, even got them laughing, to his relief, and looking at him like they knew him again.

But this didn't stop him drinking beer after beer that only kept him pissing for nothing, laughing a beat behind at every joke, his eyes jumping to the door, jumping to the door every time it opened, not for the cracker's revenge, but for the black man's; for someone, anyone to just come in and call him the asshole that he was, maybe punch him in the teeth, knock him flat, and end it with a good kick to the side of the head.

eighteen

He wore a royal blue ski mask, and a gray sweatsuit, and it was only later, when she was speaking to the young detective who sat far and safely away, on the bright yellow couch, across the big, empty living room, that she thought of this as awfully warm attire for Alabama and wondered where anyone would find such a thing as a ski mask here, given the scarcity of mountain resorts, and the fact that the temperature hadn't even hinted at going anywhere below ninety degrees for the past two weeks. And this October. October, for God's sake.

No sweat, no sourness. He'd smelled clean, like clothing soap, like his clothes would still be warm from the dryer. She had smelled leather, too, strong and straight from the glove on the hand he'd placed over her mouth.

"Don't scream," he'd said. No worry. It hadn't even occurred to her, until by telling her not to, he'd reminded her she could. She only opened her mouth against the concave of his palm, and said, "Just please don't hurt my daughter," knowing that he wouldn't, but saying it anyway, because given the situation, it seemed like something she ought to say, the right thing to do. What would later be considered admirable. But she had no doubt: it was she, he wanted.

Or maybe just wanted to think about, get closer to than on the other side of the window, where he'd probably been during the interminable length of Mr. Magoo. Between the bushes and the glass, watching mother, watching daughter, watching mother. Stroking, stroking, but holding back, holding back, and glad he had when he saw her get up and take the baby upstairs, and when he found the kitchen door to be open.

Maybe he'd not wanted this surprise as much as she hadn't, everything being muffled by the monstrous double-duty fans she'd set up to bolster the air conditioning gone breathless from too much overtime. It might have been he'd not heard her on the carpeted stairs, had been so far gone in ecstatic fancy that he did not notice her voice grow louder as she drew nearer saying, "Don't you get out of bed now. Don't you dare, Lithe Babineau. I swear, I'm not coming up there again. Not tonight," until, on the third-to-last step, she finally turned her head from the direction she wished her voice to go, to the direction her body was going and saw him, not two feet away, a thing so unexpected, so unfathomable, standing right there at the foot of the stairs inside her house, it took a long moment of upheld breath for her to believe it.

And then she ran. For the door. And immediately found all her motion to be suspended, her face facing the wall that the steps climbed above her, and saying into a hand that she would keep quiet, she promised, then nobly pleading for the safety of her child, while feeling something as strange as — relief. No more decisions to make. No more choices to weigh. No risk of failing to act, or acting on failure. As it was, by her own capture, she'd been released; her life was his now, so all she had to do, was his will.

nineteen

Poor Little Cabbage. My poor Little Cabbage," Babineau said, stroking her hair, propped by pillows and otherwise supine and bare chested, while she sat fully clothed on the side of the bed, leaning down, forehead pressed to the center of his chest where she'd put it to cry. "Poor, poor Little Cabbage. Had I only come sooner. But no. I was out defending insouciant black men from the drunken grips of the White-Trash race, and not my Little Cabbage. My sweet and good woman."

"It's okay," she said, so muffled he could barely hear.

"No. No it's not. It's fucking tragic," and he went on to bemoan his timing, early enough to have prevented the unthinkable. Too late to have brought the fucker to justice.

As would have the .45. Swiftly, obliging caliber that it was, which was why he'd lost precious moments to go and get it, rather than risk more derision that night with respect to Minnie Mouse, the bite-sized .22, and by doing so, had lost him. Hadn't even come close.

Close, only when he hadn't known it, when he'd driven up on his routine arrival home from his post-class bar-meet to see nothing but Ellie, running from porch to car, from car to porch, back to car, saying Babineau, Babineau, Babineau, like she had news so stupendous as to render her speechless. Money, he'd thought. I won something; and by the dint of that possibility, momentarily forgot he'd been set to recount his own big news of adventure.

Instead, he jumped out of the car to hear hers, and was actually smiling when he'd rounded the rear fender, saying, "What, L. C.? What is it, L. C.? Tell me."

Even by then, most likely the psychopathic bastard was far from reach, long gone across the parking lot that flanked their house — the size of two football fields, filled every home game weekend by the nationwide fans' humming R.V.s and their airhorn renditions of "Dixie" — but empty this night. Just flat open expanse, which would have had to have reduced the guy's strategic defense to the duck-and-weave and a good head start. Such a good start ahead, that Babineau hadn't a real reason to chase him, but that he wanted to and his adrenaline was pumped to make him.

So he'd run, waving around the .45 that made every good citizen in sight of it hit the deck. Pretty amusing when he described it again and again back at the bar he'd practically just left, arriving this time with Lithe and Ellie in tow, the only thing he could think to do once the detectives were done and gone.

"Come on, L. C.," he'd said. "Come on now. Be good to get out amongst friends. Have a good shot of something strong. I mean what are we going to do here? Sit on our duffs and go over the details?" Exactly what he was afraid of, and what he wanted at all costs to avoid, considering the way she was acting. So quiet, but not in her usual zip-lipped way. More like her larynx had been removed, or her left frontal lobe: silence that was the result of something missing. It scared him. She scared him. "Let's go, L. C.," and thank God she'd consented. Had ended up sitting at a table all night, surrounded by the womenfolk, which had seemed apt to him. Tribal.

"It's okay," she said again, in response to yet another flight of self-castigation, this time turning her head, so he could hear it loud and clear, or so she could breathe.

"No it's not, L. C., and it never will be," he said. "I fucked up. I fucked up good again, as usual."

But this time she didn't take the cue, and puzzled, he remembered that really, she wasn't compelled to, since it'd been she who'd come for comfort first. Bursting into tears, this time about an earring. Lost somehow going or coming from dropping Lithe at her daily lock-up. But he'd known, of course — congratulating himself on this demonstration of interpretive sensibility worthy of the female sex — that this disproportionate flood of emotion was a form of catharsis, a symptom of PTS from the previous evening's events.

"Go ahead," he said, feeling magnanimous, "just cry it out, Baby." Waiting, then relieved to hear a sniffle because he'd realized as he said it, he wasn't sure she still was.

PTS or not though, what was going on that she kept losing valuables? Either she was growing more absentminded than she normally was, maybe a full moon, or she'd fallen under some kind of curse, the long drawn-out kind, favored by the worst of fairy-tale godmothers, who preferred to dole out misfortune in slow succession, over years. How would it go? he thought, petting her hair: The Jewish American Princess, slowly stripped of all title and fortune, lives chastened by poverty, humbled ever after by lowliness, in the deep, deep South.

Couldn't help but smile at the thought. Maybe it'd make her crack one, too, once she'd dried her eyes and fixed her face.

twenty

I want to go home," she said, and heard him say, "Jesus, can't a man shit in peace?"

"Babineau. I mean it," she said, then heard a sound that confirmed he was well engaged in the activity, peace or not. Particularly obnoxious, it sounded intentionally designed to expel her from the vicinity, but she stood her ground. There were worse things, and over time she'd adapted for the sake of marital discussion. No phone he could answer. No calls he could make, no student willing to walk through this open door he made his policy. No teaching buddy coming here to share a six-pack. No waiter, no waitress to banter with, no radio for a ball game or country-western, no tapedeck for Sinatra. The only music, that of his own making. Intermittent, grotesque, noxious, but harmless to all but the weak of stomach, which was one thing Ellie did not have.

"Listen to me, Babineau. I've thought about this."

"Thought about where my boy and his girl will sleep? How they'll feel when you crash their carnal nest? For all intents and purposes, our house is theirs, L. C., for the full three months we agreed to be down here, and so I ask you, where are they gonna sleep?"

"I don't know, Babineau."

"Send them below decks to the marshy basement?"

"No. I wouldn't do that. I mean I could sleep on the couch, I guess. And Lithe has her own room."

"Oh. Of course. Lithe, too," he said, and punctuated this remark with another explosion.

"Well, I can't exactly leave her."

"And how are you two girls going to get there? Click your heels? Who pays for the airfare?"

"I don't know. Visa, I guess."

"Visa paid my way down here. Reserve credit yours, no? Any other suggestions?"

"We haven't reached the limit."

"And you want to? So we go home as broke as when we got here, maybe dug a little deeper. Could have just stayed broke in New England, fucked this honorable chairship gig." She heard him grunt, and the result of his effort.

"Babineau," she said, and sat on the end of the bed, and took a breath, knowing that if she cried, this would escalate into a sure fight. "I'm just afraid here now. All the time," and a little quaver on "time" might have given her away. "I hate it here. I mean, I like the food, and our friends. There are some things I like. But after this, I just want to go home."

"Hey, L. C. There's no safe place."

"Why don't you want me to go? Why, Babineau? Why can't I just go?" she said, and knew right then the discussion was over, and that it had never really been a discussion from the start, more like a request for permission, denied.

"Family's got to stay together. For better or worse. You know that, Little Cabbage," he said and flushed, the toilets in this house, so thunderous in their zeal they traumatized Lithe, and left no doubt that whatever went down them was never coming back.

He bought her a gun. A nickel-plated .38 that she said looked bald, because it was hammerless. Better, he said, so it would not get caught on anything, and cock mistakenly, say, in her purse. Which was where she carried it when she went outside. And in a leather clip holster when she was alone in the house with Lithe, feeling slightly crazy, a little paranoid with the weight of the thing pulling down the elasticized waistband of her raggedy gym shorts. But she wore it nevertheless.

"See there?" he said standing in the dump where they'd gone to shoot at cans and the kind of poster-sized human silhouette she'd only seen before in police movie target-practice scenes. He'd bought it at the gun shop, along with the gun and a box of bullets, one of which lay now in the center of the palm he reverentially held out to her. It was brass, shiny, almost pretty, like something that might make a chic pendant. "Hollow point. You know what it does, L. C.?" She shook her head. "Enters the individual who has had the audacity to threaten your safety and well-being, and — *boom!* — explodes. You see, we ain't fuckin' around, L. C.," and he smiled, and she smiled, and one of his students, who'd come along to shoot, too, and hold his hands over Lithe's ears when Ellie shot and Babineau coached, he smiled too, like they were making some collusive pact. Outlaws, all three.

Turned out, she was such a good shot that the silhouette he'd tacked to the one surviving tree in a landscape literally laid to waste hung tattered in no time, one big hole where once had been the torso, as if, in fact, it had been blown out from the inside. "Amazing," he said. "She is cool," he said to his student. "Isn't she a cool-handed gun-slinging babe?" he said smiling, then reached out and with his fingertips pushed her muzzle earthward, walked to the target, and tearing it down said, "We could hang this thing from our front door, Miss L. C., and ain't no one gonna fuck with you again." And turning to walk back to her, he said, "See? You didn't have to go home. You just had to start packin' iron. Ain't that right, Geoffrey?" he said to the student.

And as much as it gave her some sense of safety when she was in the house alone, or out on the street passing every man who could have been him, and as much as she liked the shine of it, the cold and solid heft of it in her hands that made her know it was as scarily real and live as surely as the weight of something dead makes it nothing else but that, she could not summon much affection for it, or admiration, or fascination. Didn't come close to becoming anything like a gun buff, and never went target shooting again, though it couldn't be disputed that she had a knack. Everytime she touched it, it felt as unfamiliar to her as it had the first time, like it was an object given her by a far-off and primitive tribe, something exhumed at an archaeological dig. It was nothing that was nor ever would be part of her frame of reference. Only his.

twenty-one

There will be a day when Gerard Babineau takes his fist and makes it go bam, bam, bam, in the center of Ellie Rifkin's face. This is after he has squeezed her neck one-handed, hard enough to obstruct the free flow of air, long enough to make her think he won't let go, and in response to her pep rally cry of: Do it! Do it! Do it!

Ever accommodating, she knelt at the edge of the mattress, now raised on a new frame she'd bought to facilitate his transfer to the chair, and bore her neck to him, gauging his reach so he'd have every opportunity to get a good grip, which he gets and keeps, staring straight into her eyes and only releasing her once it's clear she's good and scared.

But his arm, rigid and extended, has in fact been holding her up, so its removal causes her to plunge forward and fall face first into his lap. And it's while she attempts to extricate herself from this complicated position, wheelchair arm under her stomach, legs still on the bed, left arm reaching to boost herself out, and face raised to see where she is, and what she's doing, that she feels something collide with it, so fast, and so hard, she makes no sound but maybe an "oh" or an "ugh" and can't think to think of what it might have been, feels only a buzziness spreading all over the surface of her face, and funneling through and right down in, to buzz at the center of her brain. Only a slight ache where — *bam!* —

there comes another one, like its purpose is to snap her out of it, because precisely on impact she knows suddenly and absolutely what is happening, and screams, "What are you doing? What are you doing?" and twists and tries to raise her arms to block the next one which arrives just as fast and hard as the two preceding it, and pitches them both forward, sends them sliding down, as apparently the weight of his blows upon the weight of her, upon him, upon the chair, has caused the chair to tip, they tipping with it, and everything ending up on the bedroom floor; stopped, not by the pileup, but by what suddenly rises fountainlike from the center of her face. Like he'd been pounding one, two, three, on a valve and now open, it spouts a deluge, stunning in its brightness, in its quantity, in the reach of its circumference, for in moments it is all over — her, of course, but him, too, his hair, his beard, his shoulders, his chest, so on first glance it would be hard to find the origin, to know exactly whose blood it was. Until Ellie wails, "You broke my nose! You son of a bitch! You son of a bitch! You broke my fucking nose!" And something in the way she says it. Something in the sound, would make anyone believe for a moment, that there was nothing worse to break than this.

He doesn't, though. Lucky for her. Fact is, he leaves not a mark. Not even a blackened eye. And if she hadn't had to breathe through her mouth for days after, hadn't seen the blood spots that turned iodine yellow after a number of cycles in the wash, on the white cotton nightgown she liked too much to throw away, she might have wondered if the whole thing had really happened.

But there was still more for her to recall. For instance, how she really couldn't leave him on the floor — leaning against the overturned wheelchair, blood bespattered and saying over and over again how thankful he was to God that Lithe had not awakened to see this — only temporarily leaving him to take the two half-full urinals, which had fallen off the wheelchair and were dribbling into the carpet, down the hall to the bathroom where she emptied and rinsed them and then stopped for a good, careful examination of her nose, which the mirror showed to her relief did not look any different now from how it had looked before.

It just wouldn't stop bleeding, that's all, the toilet tissue fast growing soggy on her return trip to the bedroom where she found him, of course, just where she'd left him.

So what to do but right the chair, check the brake levers, and haul him into it; and what next, but to clean him up. Like she's cleaned the sweat, the urine, the shit, the holes in his legs. Now why not her blood? Why not her own blood? Washing it from him as it still drips from her, and back onto him again, the process futile. A futile one, pretty futile, wouldn't you say? Certainly taking far longer to complete than it really should.

twenty-two

It is still hot in Alabama, but Ellie will not be deterred. There to stay, might as well make the most of it, was her way of thinking. So on this, a hotter Saturday it would turn out than most of those that came before it, she decided to go sightseeing. She and Lithe, and if he woke up, Babineau, which didn't seem likely, given that Ellie's best efforts at making no effort to be quiet had caused nary a breach in the force and thunder of his snores. Flush went the toilet, shriek went the faucet, and she held Lithe's daily morning shoe-fight not a foot from his left ear. Who cared? Insomnia be damned. What gave him the right to sleep when the rest of the world didn't, those who actually got up with their children in the morning? At the very least she might cop a twitch, at best a groan and slow flop from sunny-side up to over easy. But nothing. No more than an eyelid come unhinged to show the thing beneath it roll around in there like an eight ball's oracle, revealing just what she was up against. No ordinary sleep, this, more like a neural disorder. A seizure. Not quite dead, but pretty near.

"Fuck it," she muttered, and Lithe's sneakers tied tight enough to risk gangrene, she picked her up and was out of there.

And on her way to see the ghost in the window; what Babineau's students had called it, when one night at the bar, they'd urged her to go. Story went he'd been lynched. Held in the courthouse of the town she was headed for, and a mob had come and got him. But his face, they said, was still there. Everyone could see it, in the pane of the second-floor west corner window. *Everyone,* they said, smiling, their eager assurance unwittingly raising her skepticism. Could be some scheme dreamed up by the town fathers to wring tourist revenue out of gullible Yankees, she thought — as she was of the opinion that real ghosts were not permanent fixtures, like museum inventory, but elusive, and far more discerning, choosing to reveal themselves only to those privileged enough to be able to see them. Like Babineau's ghosts: the sailor aboard ship that Babineau suddenly saw standing in his quarters when he'd turned the light off to get some shut-eye, and the long-dead owner of a bed-and-breakfast, rattling chain locks and clomping around in the wee hours, until Babineau told him he ought to be more hospitable — their manifestations previously witnessed by only a handful who, like Babineau, must have been born with the capacity to traverse worlds, while Ellie was stuck fast in this one, confined to the earthly like someone under house arrest. So given the widespread renown of this particular ghost, you could say she was on a kind of pilgrimage, a tour that was custom-made for those, like her, whose spirits were hopelessly provincial.

It began on roads that were straight and only straight, that took her past mini-mall, upon mini-mall, to ground gouged red and raw for the making of more mini-malls, to a chain-linked fenced-in local airstrip, with the kind of twelve-seaters in its hangars she knew would have flown her to Atlanta or Birmingham for a direct flight home. So her eyes lingered a bit long and longingly on this point of interest, until it gave over to agriculture. Rows and rows of short, spiky, black-stemmed, leafless plants with bits of white stuck like wet toilet paper all over them. Cotton. That's what it was. It must be cotton. Wow, she thought, no question she was in the South now. "Lithe, look," she said. "That's how cotton grows," and Lithe raised her chin, craned her neck to try for a glimpse around the blinderlike sides of her massive car seat, but did not go so far as to remove her thumb from her mouth and the scrap of cloth that had once been Raggedy Ann's apron from beneath her nose, as if she knew better than to make a real effort, whatever her mother was telling her to look at by this time, already long gone.

And all there was was woods, the road Ellie drove on between them now, the last remaining representation of human venture. Human existence, it felt like to her after a while, the only other ones around being those, like her, in moving cars. And as anonymous as this made them, it did offer Ellie some comfort, for they had to be coming from somewhere, going to someplace. Still, though, if she'd see a gas station, she'd have stopped to find out just exactly where and what and how far those places might be.

But there was no gas station, no nothing for miles, but green and trees and the road that didn't waver between them. Nothing could be that straight, that flat for that long, it seemed to her, without something diverting it. Some fissure or hump in the geography, but the monotony was relentless, and it made her feel like she was not moving at all, like all sounds and sensations that made her feel she might be were illusionary, as was the place she'd come from and the town she sought. And the only thing that would happen would be a sputter of the engine to the terminal quiet of its failure and a sense of diminishing speed as she coasted to a final stop.

Stranded. With two boxes of Berry Berry imitation fruit juice and a half a package of peanut butter Ritz Bits. Great, she thought. What would Babineau say? Proper Prior Planning Prevents Piss Poor Performance. That's what he'd say.

But this *had* to be the road. Hell, she was a better reader of maps than Babineau with all his past instruction and drills. He got lost in hotel corridors, for God's sake. Had to be pointed in the right direction when he got off an elevator. There had been two roads. Both straight, one intersecting the first, requiring a simple left-hand turn to put the town dead ahead. She wasn't stupid. And she wasn't going to pull over in the middle of nowhere to check the map again. The only thing she hadn't calculated was scale, and so maybe her time approximation was a little off, and it was as simple as that.

But for all her attempts at confidence, her relief at seeing a sign confirming her arrival at the right place, or anywhere at all, for that matter, nearly necessitated an unscheduled rest stop, so she could get a grip on herself. But instead, she reached over and took Lithe's small, soft hand, no longer so scared now, as to be unable to appreciate the sweet baby-squish still left in the wrist. "We made it," she said, and was in and nearly out of the town square, nearly past the town hall, before she knew it, and had to take a fast turn to stay there, and start looking for a place to park, the curbside parking so plentiful, she wondered if it were allowed, until she had to figure this was not the kind of town that would need to impose stringent regulations for unimpeded traffic flow, since there was no traffic, the roads were dirt, and coming into town, she'd had to steer around a big, yellow dog who'd been lying stretched to the full, right in the middle of the street.

What am I doing? she thought on her second rotation and yanked the car to the curb.

The engine off, she paused to appreciate the very last of the cool air it had manufactured before it would be infused with what lay beyond the sealed windows, looking pretty brutal in the noon-day sun.

"Out, Mommy. I want to get out," Lithe said, holding the sides of her car seat, pushing on her hands, swinging her feet up, and crashing them down again.

"Okay. Okay. Hold your horses," Ellie said. She opened the car door, and was once again amazed, as well as bored, with how amazed she could still be by the kind of hot hot was in this part of the country. Lithe was not going to like it, but Ellie'd no choice but to unbuckle, lift, transfer Poody from hand to pocket, and set her down, only noticing then, how deserted things felt, how loud the slam of the car door sounded. It was more than just no traffic. There were no people. Houses, yes, with those low-sloped porch roofs, windows far back in the gloom beneath them, looking opaque, like one-way mirrors through which all the people who she couldn't see were looking at her. The only living thing she actually *had* seen since she got there, she realized, had been that dog, who on second thought, might not have just been sleeping. Had she driven into the middle of a B horror film? Stumbled onto some terrible government secret? Did this town even exist? And just when she'd spooked herself thoroughly, she did see some real-live people looking right at her from across the town green that was mined with the red-clay hills of fire ants. Three elderly black men in jeans and plaid shirts who stood absolutely still beneath a big, maybe an oak, tree, like they were trying for camouflage, looking at that dumb, fat-thighed white woman tourist, come here all by herself with that baby girl to observe their town like it was some carnival diorama, is what she saw from what she could see in their faces at her distance. What in hell she want with us?

She smiled and waved and they just looked, did not make a move, so if she were going to accomplish what she came there for, she'd have to rudely turn her back on them to look where she'd been told, and wondered if they knew about the ghost in the window, too, if they were figuring that that was why she was there, and if they thought it a pretty stupid thing to come all this way to see, to come all this way based on the contents of an apocryphal story. Pretty silly. Childish even. What an idiot, she thought — until she faced the closed-up looking building, and not sure which window was the west one, looked.

It was not three-dimensional, nothing that would suddenly swoop out at her like Casper. It could have been a fluke in a configuration of ice crystals, the handiwork of Jack Frost — if the temperature wasn't what it was — something that caught light to show the grooves and creases that unmistakably made a brow, a nose, lips, the line of a jaw. And she knew, no question, this was not an elaborate trick, nor an imperfection in the window glass. It was an imprint, like a fossil, or an old photonegative plate, evidence of something that had once been alive: this man, his face and the very last look he'd cast from it down upon those who'd come to get him.

"Wow," she said softly. Then said, "Look, Lithe, look. See it?" and squatted to point. And Lithe gave it a good go. Looked up somewhere in the vicinity and said a tentative "yeah," trying, Ellie knew, to please her crazy mother, unaware of what she was supposed to be looking at, and obviously seeing nothing.

"The face," Ellie said. "See it?" realizing that Lithe would be her only witness, providing sole proof for Babineau that she wasn't lying, or elaborating on an optical illusion, knowing he'd smile that indulgent smile, loath to believe she was capable of any communication with anything remotely connected to the supernatural. Just an old land-dwelling creature was she, crawled out from the sea, but gone no further than that on the evolutionary scale. "Lithe. Look. See?" she said, her voice near to cracking.

"Mommy, I'm hot," Lithe said, and Ellie knew that was it. Next would be the request to go home, and she really couldn't blame her. It was hellish there.

part three

twenty-three

Wouldn't you know it would be a cat would lead to his undoing, another grand alteration of Babineau's life. Black, with a little white, stuck in the very same tree it got stuck in two times before. Only this time it was higher, and the windchill was a good ten degrees subzero, and like each time previous, no kindly fire fighter was going to risk his neck to bring it down. No, that would best be done with a .22 caliber bullet. High degree of difficulty, but not impossible, not impossible, Babineau thought, looking up at the mewing carcass every time he passed it going to class and coming from, even pausing once to aim a finger and go *pow!*

So imagine his delight when he was literally handed the job, the owner drawn, as she must have been by his reputation alone, to knock on his door and offer it to him. "Yes," he said. "Certainly. I'd be pleased to. Honored," he said in true gentleman-gunfighter fashion — more words than he'd said to her in all her first three months of faculty meetings and cross-campus nods, as she was not exactly his next-in-line candidate for a drinking buddy — the brand-new comparative lit teacher who hailed from the far northern regions of Maine, and who was, without a doubt, a very odd duck.

Stomped for a walk, head tucked, as if for incoming, and eyes straight down on the hiking boots she wore with long, woolen skirts, tights, baggy old sweaters, and a jacket that looked like she pumped it each morning with free air from the outdoor hose at the local filling station; nothing in her attire that hinted at a color brighter than gray, and all topped, of course, with academic-issue horn-rims and a never-been-fucked look that would have rivaled the Virgin Mary if it wasn't for the fact of her children.

Two of them. Girls, and pale. Pale hair, pale skin, pale lips, pale eyes. Probably be white at the quick of their nails, like they'd been long submerged. Hatched — that was it — from egg clusters to swim round and round until they sprouted legs.

"I believe my cat is retarded," the woman said sadly, clearly in need of his concurrence, which he readily provided, along with a tactfully stated inquiry as to a time and date best suited to spare her children any unwarranted trauma.

"That's very thoughtful of you," she said, obliged him with one, and business thus concluded, he was hightailing it down to the bedroom — Ellie calling — What? What was that about? — where he began to disassemble, oil and clean, reassemble, spin, snap, sight, and dry fire his instrument of execution before the front door had completed its slow, closing arc.

This was when he and Ellie were living on campus in the same senior housing turned faculty housing he'd inhabited with wife number two. This house identical, but for its orientation to the path of the sun, and a floor-wide covering of blue instead of red carpet, left mercifully unmolested by a warehouse worth of fine antiques. Space is what they wanted and what they got, no denying, related in part to Ellie's all-fired desire for a baby to put in it.

"Woman wants a baby, woman she gets a baby," Babineau said to Borger's alarm at this next fast turn his life was bound to take. "Comes with the territory," he said, and tossed back a bourbon he would follow with many, so as to come home that night, full of loud sentiment and drunken expansiveness to wake his sleeping bride and promise her ten, twelve, all the little babies her heart desired. He would provide.

But after six months of sex on command, he wasn't so sure. Not his fault he knew, as he had four of his bloodline walking the earth to prove it, begotten by the very unreliability of the Rhythm Method. "Problem is," he said, "you're trying too hard, L. C. You want it too much. Got to be like me and wife number one. Fucked like rabbits with every intention of not killing one and there they came, voluntarily stepping up for the slaughter three years in a row, a little lag time and then a fourth." He'd attributed it all to God's will, though wife number one, on the third or fourth test positive — he couldn't remember — had tried to deny it, and said she wasn't any goddamn Catholic to begin with. But, of course, eventually she'd got calmed down.

And sure enough, Ellie conceived sometime within the month they were otherwise preoccupied by the worst fight so far of their marital life. The result of an impromptu party that turned ugly enough to draw Ellie from her downstairs sanctum, foolishly place herself in the middle of the fray, and order everyone out, including him. And when he laughed and stood his ground, she did her best throw-yourself-at-him maneuver and then admirably ducked his self-defensive swing to retreat herself, no change of clothes, no toothbrush, no clue as to where she'd disappeared to for two terrible days and three worse nights, until in the early morning of the third, she entered the darkened bedroom like a sylph, and lay down beside him, heard his plea and his sorrow and granted him absolution, while neither knew at the time, she was two weeks gone with child. Positively biblical, he was to say, something right out of her very own testament.

So that's why they were living there, and the cat was why they were soon to live there no longer. Because he got it, all right, and what a pretty shot it was, his only regret being that no one was around to witness it: up through twelve or thirteen branches, in the tricky light of dusk, the target a virtual silhouette, but fairly stable, as the thing had to be by then half-frozen, and was sure enough dead before it crish-crashed, wump and bumped to land thump on the ground. Not even an involuntary twitch to indicate how recently alive it had been.

Fortunate, since the sound of gunfire had drawn the owner from her home, whereupon she'd stopped short at the corpse to pronounce Sneakers, Snookers, no, Socks, or whatever — a good cat. Babineau fearing then the moment she'd turn on him, batter her fists on his chest, and cry foul. For women were capable of anything, all the contradictory messages he was getting from Ellie enough to set his head to spinning Exorcist-style, like nothing he could do was right, even if he did what she said was right for him to do. So to forestall any hysterical outburst, he said in his smoothest, most sweetest, most Mel Torme-ish voice, "Jody, you did him a favor. We just sped up the nature of natural selection, is all. He wasn't long for this world."

And she agreed and thanked him and left Babineau to rest on his laurels, enjoying, more than he'd imagined, the angel of mercy role: feet spread, gun smoking, woman crying gratitude and grief before him. So it would only follow, of course, that like any of the James Dean antiheroes he'd emulated as a boy, he'd eventually be run out of town.

By the authorities, who with little ceremony, after his twenty-two years of underpaid devotion to a thankless profession, asked him to move off campus. Oh, we still want you to *teach* for us, they'd said, while we render you and your wife and child home-less. Conscience-free it seemed to him, shaking his hand with practiced cordiality, this new slick politician of a president and his sidekick female dean, who, of the two of them, was the one had the shiny brass balls. Teach for them his ass. Sure, he'd move off campus. Ellie got her trust fund, thanks to Grandma, and he the twenty thou from his mother's estate. No way would his persecu-tors continue to capitalize off his national renown, the fact that he put this second-rate institution on the map. "Fuck it, Little Cabbage," he said to his silent wife. "I'm gonna retire."

Turned out, though, retirement was not all it was cracked up to be. He thought he would sit at his desk, gaze out upon the land he owned like a corrupt and indolent nobleman, and write brilliant tracts, devise new theories, shake up the political scene, while his blood pressure dove down to normal. But all he could do was hustle for a buck, hustle for a buck, accept every gig and offer that came his way like a two-bit whore, not about to quibble over price. Ellie's tutoring barely bringing in a dime, his retirement pension about enough to keep an eighty-year-old geezer in public housing. He had to put food on the table and fill the mouth of a child that seemed never to close — as much as he loved her — the noise factor enough to drive him, as it often did, out of the house and down to his new local bar where he'd buddy up with the latest motorcycle gang or grab a corner stool and utter to any within hearing the infamous line of every male bonding movie he ever did like: "I'm too old for this shit. I'm too old for this shit. I'm too old, I'm too old, I'm too old for this shit."

twenty-four

B abineau. Concentrate on your lungs," she says, leaning close to his ear, speaking to him the way she would were he trapped beneath debris, or at the foot of a well-hole, attempting to divert him, calm him, offer instruction until the rescue team arrived. "Concentrate on your lungs," she says, can only hope he comprehends and will trust that there's some logic to this command, enough to follow it like a good lieutenant would his ranking officer.

Of course it's the mind over body thing, so she figures he'll catch on. Trendy, she knows, touted recently by a number of best-sellers on the subject, but, hey, it's another strategy, a relief from her generous plea bargains with the supposedly Divine. Now she pictures the striated, maroon, plastic organ, easily removed and replaced in the chest cavity of her high school science lab's ghoulish model of a human's upper half. Thinks of white bits of bone marrow, coursing the bloodstream's surface like Styrofoam, swirling in eddies, stuffing those crucial capillaries. And she tells it to get lost.

Which it does — eventually, his respiratory improvement confirmed by visual record on the X rays the doctors raise to the nearest overhead with flourish and the sound of buckling sheet metal. Only on film it does not resemble her version of *The Incredible*

Journey. No, it looks more like smoke, and in sequential shots, like the dissipation of morning mist. And this seems right to her. That it's not a sudden miracle, but a response — to a few degrees of temperature, a shift in the alignment of Earth to Moon. Tide drops. Fog lifts. Rain stops. Babineau lives.

twenty-five

She was sorry for the land, and she didn't know exactly how she'd come to be putting a house on it. Too little land and too many houses already, in her opinion, and now here she was, going to build another one — that looked kind of like a trailer, she'd say, quick to beat any visitor to the observation: students, faculty, friends, a campus security guard or two, who'd inevitably find themselves looking at page fourteen of the builder's big brochure. Ellie'd be damned if they were going to think for a second that the house pictured there would ever be her preferred aesthetic choice. "You know, economics," she'd say, figuring anyone could understand *that*. And before they dared make the next assumption, she'd tell them — no, it was not a prefab, but a kit house, though had she been asked to elaborate on the difference, her explanation might have grown a bit sketchy. Something to do with the former requiring little more than a level and a staple gun for assembly, while the latter might be more traditionally constructed with hammer and nail. But then Babineau would inevitably come along and ruin everything with an excited depiction of how it was shipped: "Loaded in its entirety on the flatbed of an eighteen-wheeler, precut, premeasured, right down to the studs and drywall," he'd say, as though suddenly he was some kind of an expert, and thus undermine all her efforts to convince any who'd shown a hint of interest that this was quality construction, for certainly she'd be skeptical of a house ordered by number and delivered like a high-end item from a hobby-shop catalog.

"Might even throw in the waterfall, heh, heh, heh," said the builder, jovially referring to the one so meticulously and convincingly rendered by the brochure artist it was hard to imagine the house without it roaring down those moss-covered rocks, not an arm's length from the corner of the sundeck "the size of a football field," the builder had thundered, a man who wouldn't have denied throwing 'round the pigskin himself a time or two — like Ellie and Babineau were really the football-flyrod types, ironically purchasing the one house of the twenty-four offered, purported to be the outdoorsman's ideal hideaway, and boasting a kitchen sized to fit a double-burner hot plate, indispensable for the heating of that hearty woodsman's can o' beans fare.

"But it's got a cathedral ceiling," the builder was quick to point out. And the word packed just the punch it was meant to, conjuring images of Chartres, of Notre Dame, and finally swaying Ellie to admit that, yes, it was all pretty exciting, her very own house after all, lots of triple-paned thermal-glass windows, and prefinished hardwood floors, clean geometric lines, and a view from three-quarters up the hill of pastureland and grazing cows that would rival any come-to-New-England promo shot. So when the builder rose and kept rising from behind his equally oversized desk to extend his catcher's mitt hand, they didn't hesitate to grab it and one, then the other, shake the deal done.

Only the land gave her pause, for it was beautiful and the house was not, and there was no question in Ellie's mind as to who should be the one to claim it. Not her of course, but the things that already had: the spreading juniper, poplar trees, maple saplings, sumac, and all manner of wildflowers and meadow grass, everything that years ago blew in on the wind and saw opportunity in this abandoned cow pasture to germinate and flourish and provide home and habitat to so many living things. Even the rock she sat on, surely left there by a glacier, in one day's time doomed to a three-second burial beneath the caterpillar wheels of two roaring 'dozers. But she would not be witness. Instead she'd come as she had, beforehand, climbing the hill on impulse to pay homage, offer her thanks, and beg for forgiveness, while Babineau waited in the car, waited and waited until he could wait no longer and honked the horn, and yelled up to her, asking what the hell was she doing, and would she please hurry the fuck up.

When, if she'd bothered to tell him, he could have easily avoided all this rigmarole by telling her, as he would eventually anyway, that she was wasting her time, that nature was far more resilient and far less forgiving than she still so childishly believed. For sure enough, whether it was revenge or the cold scientific properties of gravity, the moment that house was up, nature did its damnedest to knock it right down again.

"Yep," one workman was to say, "water and gravity, home owner's two most formidable enemies." Maybe it was the guy who'd come to fill the two-foot deep, three-foot wide trench carved by runoff into the crest of the unpaved driveway, providing Ellie with a fine teaching tool to demonstrate for Lithe the amazing erosive power of water, or an example of the kind of fissure one might see as the result of a shift in the earth's continental plates.

Or maybe, no, it was not the driveway guy who said it, but the one who'd come on emergency notice to pump out the basement. Yes, it was him — comfortably sloshing around in his thigh-high waders, attaching hose to hose with a deftness that barely required his attention, while he affably pointed out every monumental and irreversible blunder she and Babineau had made when it came to the construction of their home, starting with their builder, who everyone but they, it seemed, knew was an unremittent crook.

Easy for him to say, she thought, when he could slosh right on out of here, climb into his stupid little truck, and drive away — that is, if there was a driveway left to drive on — while what could she do, but stay there, right where she was, right where she'd gone to survey the damage, standing one mere step above a water level, which was, he laconically, slosh, slosh, informed her, still rising.

twenty-six

She tells him she doesn't love him anymore and knows why the innocent crack under interrogation, that lightbulb above their head, blindfold over the eyes, hands and feet tightly bound.

"Say it you lying bitch," he says. "You know it's the truth. Just say it. Say it," he says until she screams, "Okay. Okay. Maybe I don't. I don't *know*. I don't *know*, Babineau," she says, the tears up and running into the terrible silence that follows. Now he can do anything to her he wants because she's hurt him enough to deserve it. And when she dares glance at him, he's smiling, actually smiling, well more of a grimace really, the expression on the face of a man about to run his lifelong nemesis through.

So why won't he? Why won't he just do it now? Stick her and dump her in a back alley — that doesn't exist, no dirty basement either, soundproofed and window-blacked for the purposes of covert activity. No, they're in a car, Babineau at the wheel, driving down a road, the rural road they live on, where she runs and bikes, Lithe on the back saying, "Not too bumpy, Mommy. Not too bumpy." And it's a beautiful day, early summer, the shadow sun shadow sun coursing over the windshield like river water. There's a field, a cemetery, pastureland, a grazing bay-colored horse, the farmstand she visits nearly every other day where she buys those honey sticks for Lithe and radishes just because they're so fat and red.

And she realizes, my God, he aims to spare her, he's going to spare her. He'll let her go, oh, merciful, merciful one. Remove the blindfold, loose the ropes gently, gently, then step back, arms folded, legs spread, to watch, and see how far she gets. How far, before she falls down, gets up, falls down, gets up, falls down and doesn't get up. Stays down, alive, still breathing, breathing, but not for long, not for long now, waiting, just waiting like any other dumb and injured beast, for the end.

twenty-seven

Get vertical. You got to get vertical," the doctor says, and they think, who's he think he's kidding? One leg smashed to smithereens, the other food for the hospital furnace, a rather severe impediment to this tall order, no? "No comprende. No comprende, Il Signor Doctore," Babineau says, like he could just jump up and do the fucking jitterbug. What a joke. *Stand?* Babineau hasn't even sat, yet.

And on the day he does, it's like the earth's doing its best to pull him right back down again — at his cheeks, the rims of his eyes, pulling, pulling to keep him where it got him and do to him what it has been, more, it seems, than anything done by the impact of a car.

He looks worse than when he arrived. Diminished. Done in. Even his hair is falling out, and what has that got to do with bones? It's the lying down. It's the inactivity, the lack of resistance to the thing that keeps the heavenly bodies in their proper place. But when it comes to the human one, struck down by tragic circumstance, well, it's gravity that wreaks the most havoc; that is, till someone makes him move.

Something he most definitely does not want to do. Because it hurts, goddamn, he says. Jesus fucking Christ, he says, my fucking back is breaking. Forget it, forget it, he says to all who've come to rally him, to hoist him up and up. He looks yellow. He says he's dizzy. He says just wait, just wait a minute. So they do, and then they don't, and then one, two, three, they swing him up and over and into the chair, and everyone's clapping and everyone's cheering, and Ellie wonders, what is there to celebrate? He's crying, can't they see? Crying — those idiots, those imbeciles — far from tears of joy, it's grief she knows; she wants to yell: Grief.

twenty-eight

When Ellie Rifkin finally leaves Gerard Babineau she takes nothing with her but a small brown duffel. Same duffel, in fact, they'd received as a wedding gift that had contained items meant for a gourmet picnic on their honeymoon train ride south — caviar, pâté, cornichon pickles, maybe a bottle or two of Moët Chandon — all rolling around and banging together in there, necessitating a transfer, as she remembered, to a more appropriate container, the duffel eventually used then, for what she was using it for now: a pair of jeans, underwear, a sweatshirt, sneakers, a book — couldn't go anywhere without a book — the kind of things she might have taken on an overnight. Toothbrush, of course. But not much more than that, because her first and foremost intention was to get *herself* out of there and not anything else. To flee — as she would before a hurricane or the indiscriminate destruction of any natural disaster. The sirens were wailing, as it were, before a thing that could not be stopped. Her evacuation really, a matter of her life and her death.

No kidding. That was, pretty much what it had come down to. Ellie's recognition of this, arriving a day or so beforehand, while she lay upon the cool blue tiles of her bathroom floor, the very tiles she'd so assiduously chosen for their resemblance to the bottom of a pool, or clean ocean floor. She'd sure liked those tiles; and now she was lying on them, her view of the hanging light fixture nearly, but not completely, obstructed by the porcelain bulge of the toilet bowl that loomed above her like an amazing feat of architecture.

She'd chosen that too, the toilet — and the light fixture for the frosted shade, the antiqued brass chain, and yet it was hardly recognizable now, the dust on it thick enough to resemble silt, the whole object like a relic discovered in a chamber of a long-sunken luxury liner. Shocking. Enough to have turned Ellie's thoughts away from the ones previous that had had to do with other things related to despair, and toward the recollection of how gratified she'd been the instant she'd seen the fixture up. And yet had its maintenance even occurred to her? The fact that she could have purchased something tall enough for her to climb to reach not just the bulb, but the shade above it so as to keep it looking good as new.

The tiles too — the crumbling grout between, loosening them like ice flows. And the rest of the house — walls scraped, carpet stained, floors gouged. And what had she been doing but running around and running around, plugging this, nailing that, trying her best to batten the hatch, batten the hatch when it looked like it was her own that had finally blown.

And sent her careening, with a crash and skid, to her knees, the only place to be when the body's bent on throwing everything that's inside of it out. Her body, not her will, the thing that is breaking. And now spent, prostrate, and literally belly up, she knows she's sunk.

So next day or so, she packs a small bag, walks between Babineau and whatever video it is tonight that he watches from the couch, along with the usual conglomeration of visitors who are lying on the floor, leaning on the furniture, slouched in the rocker, like a company at ease while she boldly goes AWOL. Maybe she said good-bye, as she did think of the moment as being momentous enough to warrant it, or maybe she didn't, fearing perhaps that the soundtrack was too great a competitor and she wouldn't want to blow the moment by having to repeat herself. And after all, she hadn't used the kitchen door. They could all see what she was doing, and an hour or two earlier she'd made no secret of her plans, calmly announcing them in front of this very same audience while they ate the dinner she'd prepared, but not partaken in herself. So maybe a pause at the threshold, then nothing left but to open the door and close it behind her and be out in the night and walking down the sundeck steps to the car, just as she might have for any inconsequential errand — to pick up some milk or baby formula. Her departure, really, like any one those visitors would take at the movie's end. Unprotested, no obstacles to navigate but the few bodies she had to step over, no armlock, or body block, or confrontation with the barrel of a gun. Not even the usual firestorm of insults. She just walked to the sliding glass door, stopped, or maybe didn't, for a brief and general good-bye.

But the point is, she slid it open, and shut. Simple as that.

twenty-nine

"If you take my children, I swear to God, I'm gonna shoot you," he said pushing himself up the hallway behind her. But found it wasn't necessary, because when she did leave she didn't take them, and he thought he had it made. Abandonment. Now of all the things he thought her capable of, that hadn't been one of them. Well, woman's always full of surprises. Exactly why he should have prepared himself for the next one, when five days later she returned with the almighty piece of paper, great weapon of a supposedly civilized society, stuck in the hand of a miserable rookie cop who didn't look old enough to be carrying that .357 snapped snug in its holster and right at the level of Babineau's eyes.

He said Ellie had one, too. A .38 he bought for her in Alabama — You know how easy it is to buy a gun in Alabama? — and was stupid enough to teach her how to use it. Legal. All the papers were in order. She was licensed. So he didn't know why she was going off about all his guns when what was to prevent her from going into the closet right now, unlocking the lockbox and using hers on him. So he didn't know why *he* should be considered such a menace, as he had no prior record and had even served in this fine country's armed forces. Talking and talking because he had to keep filling time with sound while she was busy in the bedrooms, packing their things. Might as well have been sharpening a machete for the express purpose of cutting off the last of what he had that were

his balls. No snip, snip for her, but a good air-whistling wack —
that bitch — who was so self-righteously taking his children from
him, now that she thought she had the law on her side. Oh, dearly
deluded, carrying out her condoned kidnapping, law-enforced
entry; and the very youngest not even seven months old.

"I'll get them back," he said to the officer's butt, which happened to move in front of him just as he spoke. Butts, belt buckles,
that was his worldview these days, and irony of all ironies — shoes.
Ain't that a laugh, the thing he'd never wear a pair of in his life
again. Hadn't known there was such a variety and what they could
say about the owner. And now hers, walking out on him for a second time, those infernal hiking boots she always wore, as if to keep
reminding him that ever since they'd married she hadn't done one
of the things she liked best to do because he'd told her it was
ridiculous. Actually volunteering to hike fifteen miles without
some foul-mouthed drill sergeant on your ass to make you in the
hills of Quantico in 102 degrees Fahrenheit until you had to fall
back and puke. Call him certifiable, he'd said, if he ever did it when
he wasn't under orders.

Baby on her hip and Lithe on her hand, some big new duffel,
not his anyway, weighing her shoulders crooked as she went past
and he said, "I'll play your pussy-assed game of legalese bullshit
better'n you, L. C. You'll see," he said, pushing his hands down on
the arms of the chair so as to raise himself off it for some goddamn
height. Just to get some goddamn height. "And you will never see
them again. Got that L. C.? Never." And then the kitchen door
went bang, the Keystone Kop right behind her, down the four-
tiered switchback custom-made wheelchair ramp, into their get-
away cars, and down the hill.

His hill. *His* house. His fucking Northeast Kingdom, as he liked
to call it, that he would gladly rule solo from his ambulatory
throne. Fuck'er, he thought. He won't execute this with a firing
squad or one well-placed sharpshooter. He'll break out the guillo-
tine, by God, and let'er roll.

thirty

He changed the locks and put the Marine Corps hymn on the answering machine, and Ellie thought, all those months she'd bathed him, fed him, washed his hair and cleaned his wounds and soothed him when he cried.

And he so damn pious when those church ladies came in their big American cars, struggling against the grade of the hill to open those massive doors, haul themselves from the plush interior and ascend the sundeck steps to where he waited for Communion, mouth open, tongue extended, as greedy and eager as a bald little bird. Twice a day sometimes, like its effects could not outlast most of your over-the-counter painkillers. Perhaps not even longer than it took to chew and swallow. She just had to wonder about him and his God if he could sit on the bed and talk on the phone and watch her pound on the glass door, begging and begging for him to let her in, just let her in, that all she wanted was a few more clothes, just some *clothes,* for God's sake, Babineau. Was this really something Jesus would condone?

And here she'd gone and thought that they'd never been better, their union nearly divine, so strengthened as it had been by adversity, deepened by their joint ministrations to his body and equal commitment to his speedy recovery. More intimate than sex, she'd confided to some, and replete with the bonus that he'd never again have to question her devotion. For wasn't this the ultimate test? And pregnant, too, by God. Nothing like loading it on. Giving

birth by cesarean section in the middle of everything and returning home from *her* hospital stay to gamely pick up right where
she'd left off, bending over the baby now strapped onto her exte-
rior and only taking some breaks to breast-feed and even rigging
that sometimes so she could do it while still doing for others.

They'd risen to the occasion, hadn't they? Babineau, brave and
gentle and grateful, and Ellie, strong and nurturing and as selfless as
any would be in her situation. "It's just what you do," she'd say to
those who'd marveled. Her humility genuine, but nevertheless she
was pleased that it seemed they'd so swiftly passed the AP of APs of
spiritual tests. For after the first two weeks of the Why? Why? Whys?
she'd concluded that neither she nor Babineau could have committed any sin terrible enough to have brought upon themselves this
kind of punishment. Especially Babineau, whose suffering was
untoward. That would be the doings of that bad-ass Old Testament
God, as Babineau might say, who favored lightning strikes and boils
and frogs as a means of teaching his charges a lesson. That theory
rejected, it had to be they'd been chosen: their earthly task to
become better people than the ones they'd been before and thus set
an example for all, of courage, nobility, and enduring love.

"How can you do this to me?" she screamed, pounding and
pounding on the bedroom's glass door and really wanting an
answer, though all that crying and yelling would have intimidated
any willing enough to give one, which Babineau definitely was not.
"How *can* you, Babineau?" His behavior positively eerie, the way
he was watching her while still talking to someone on the phone,
like she was a drama section video pick that he'd pressed to mute.

Until finally, she gave up. One more agonized cry and a good
fist to the triple-paned glass and then she stopped, feeling like
someone was behind her; some *thing*. All that space out there: the
sky, the land, the beautiful view they'd claimed to their detriment
by building at this ridiculous elevation. She felt it was watching
her, listening with the same detachment, the same impassivity as
the man she saw before her — the whole world, clearly, what she
was up against.

thirty-one

That thing?" Babineau says when the young prosthetist bounds in with it, hefting it like a barbell, which is not so far different from what it looks like, barbell, tire iron — and not what it is, not what it could possibly be. "You've got to be kidding," Babineau says, especially after hearing from the first ranking of all the king's horses and men, way back in hospital time — that this would be his good leg, his *good* leg, he'd said.

"This has got to be some kind of joke," Babineau says, because with all the crap he's heard about aluminium pylons and duraplex sockets and a variety of knees to rival the dry goods section of any supermarket, this looked downright primitive. He was waiting for the guy to show him how it really worked, hid a camera or doubled as a blow gun, something, anything to bring it into the twentieth century. But it remained a bare rod with something at the center similar in size and technical complexity to a cabinet hinge, a cup at the top deep enough to fill with a couple of pints of Guinness (must have seen that in a movie somewhere), all cloudy-like and bumpy, like it was made of paraffin as opposed to a substance better used to watertight the hulls of America's finest speedboats. And then the thing at the bottom, attached perpendicular and shaped like something Gepetto might design for his puppet son. No toes, no arch, and made of Band-Aid tan rubber. Disgusting, appalling. "You've got to be kidding," Babineau kept saying, shaking his head and smiling like he might cry if he let his mouth do anything else. And ignoring all the prosthetist's explanations and remonstrations, along with Ellie's, who, behind him, had taken up the refrain — though earlier Babineau had noticed those eyes start to blazing and that she-lion you-fix-this-or-I'll-kill-you sound in her voice he'd come to love and depend on when it had been questionable upon their summons from waiting to examining room as to whether or not he'd be able to clear the doorway. Not a good omen for this stage of the game, they'd agreed, as this was supposed to be a medical facility of sorts, no? Or was he the only one to have ever entered this place in this advanced a state of gimpdom. Certainly miles beyond the prosthetist who was, as part of his pep talk, just now drawing up the right pant leg of his pressed khakis to reveal there the manikin sheen of a falsey that he was saying would resemble what would eventually be Babineau's after months to years of the adjustments and refinements and delays necessary to compensate for the shrinkage, blisters, and occasional infections that afflict the remainder of any limb that has lost its better half. Once that's all done with, he says, then Babineau could graduate to a cosmetic covering, soft or hard, and choose from knee designs up the wah-zoo.

Small-fry, is what Babineau thinks, looking at him, so eager and young and stupid. A chump. He and his mini-amputation. Two knees and one perfectly sound leg and the row of ribbon-hung medals he was now indicating on the wall with the grand-sweep gesture of a Vegas magician. "Yeah, I saw them. I saw," Babineau says. All awards for gimp downhill skiing competitions and one-legged water-sport meets. The very last recreations Babineau would have participated in with two legs, much less one. "Yeah, yeah. That's great," he says. "But get a load a this," he says, now doing his own little show-and-tell, barely able to contain himself, so eager is he to see the guy blanch and go speechless at the sight of the leg he does still have, or something that vaguely resembles a leg as it still seems to be attached to the hip and there, has a foot at the end of it, five toes at the tip, though the foot's got a sausage-like hue and kind of twists unbidden inward and, as Babineau explains, hasn't got some key circuits connected, the one, for instance that lifts it, so if his knee could in fact bend enough to propel him forward with that peg leg taking up the left-side slack, the right foot would plow a good long furrow behind him. "It's *this* leg, *this* leg that's cosmetic. Only good for keeping me from looking like more of a freak than I already am, eh? But still shocking, no? Still shocking in itself," he says to Mr. Athletic, leg builder of the twelfth century, a guy dense enough to go back in the water when, as he'd told it, it was an outboard motor changed the course of his life. Asshole. "So what do you think?" Babineau says, containing just barely his desire to finish off that sentence with the word he'd just thought. "Think I'll be dancing in a couple of weeks on that sorry piece of hardware? Think I'll be stalking some gray squirrels and cock pheasants in the New England wilderness before the season's out?" No, he wasn't going to listen to this secondary citizen of the monoped minority with his little below-the-knee inconvenience. Nor was he going to listen to any of those able-bodied bipeds, who seemed to be crowding the whole fucking universe, no clue as to how fortunate they were that they didn't have to piss into plastic every day of their lives because they hadn't been fool enough to take a stroll in the speed lane of an interstate at night. What had he been thinking? What had made him do it? What had been his rationale? Good Samaritan his ass. Maybe he'd thrown that woman out of the way, but he'd lured her sweet young brother right into it. Nobody. Not nobody was going to get his respect. Only those with the least leg left. That double amputee dykey-bikey girl he'd befriended at Outpatient. Or all the quads and paraplegics, all the world's unfortunates, who couldn't control their bowels or get a hard-on ever ever again. Only for them would Babineau pray. The rest, as far as he was concerned, could go to hell.

thirty-two

If only he'd taken the scenic route — was one of the many *if onlys,* along with the zillion *what ifs* that could claim the distinction of having been uttered aloud, expelled like a gumball from brain to mouth one day while she was doing the usual: folding, packing, folding, packing a noodle-length piece of peroxide soaked gauze into his leg with the dexterous manipulation of two sterile tweezers. "If *only,* Babineau," she said despite her better intentions to never dare suggest even his merest culpability.

But how could she not? How could she not wonder why he'd done what he did and wish that he'd done something else? They'd been *strangers* for God's sake, *strangers* — when he had a pregnant wife and a four-year-old at home. So when *did* his family come first? You tell her. But, of course, it had been the moment at hand, the immediate situation. Not an instance given to contemplation and the careful consideration of all potentialities. Hell, it wasn't much different from the turn of the wheel to the right or to the left. Still, she couldn't help herself, couldn't help but think what might have been, had he, for instance, taken the scenic route. But then she went and *said* it, as if he didn't have enough on his mind.

But he only said, "I know," so gently, so softly that she knew he'd thought of it, too, probably for months, most likely from the very beginning: that if he'd only taken the scenic route, if he'd only taken the scenic route, he'd have never come upon what had laid ahead.

"Oh, Babineau," she said, looking at him, and he looking at her, and neither looking away for a long time while they felt sorry, so sorry together, for what had happened to them.